OVER THE
WOODWARD WALL

OVER THE WOODWARD WALL

A. Deborah Baker

A TOM DOHERTY ASSOCIATES BOOK
New York

This is a work of fiction. All of the characters, organizations, and events portrayed in this novel are either products of the author's imagination or are used fictitiously.

OVER THE WOODWARD WALL

Edited by Lee Harris

A Tordotcom Book
Published by Tom Doherty Associates
120 Broadway
New York, NY 10271

www.tor.com

Tor® is a registered trademark of Macmillan Publishing Group, LLC.

The Library of Congress Cataloging-in-Publication Data is available upon request.

ISBN 978-0-7653-9927-4 (hardcover)
ISBN 978-0-7653-9926-7 (ebook)

Our books may be purchased in bulk for promotional, educational, or business use. Please contact your local bookseller or the Macmillan Corporate and Premium Sales Department at 1-800-221-7945, extension 5442, or by email at MacmillanSpecialMarkets@macmillan.com.

First Edition: October 2020

Printed in the United States of America

0 9 8 7 6 5 4 3 2 1

THIS BOOK IS FOR
MY CUCKOOS YET TO COME.
I HOPE I SEE YOU FLY.

OVER THE
WOODWARD WALL

ONE

THE SAME ORDINARY TOWN

In the same ordinary town, on the same ordinary street, lived two very different, very ordinary children who had never quite managed to cross paths with one another. This, too, was sadly ordinary, for the line dividing children who went to *this* school from children who went to *that* school ran right down the middle of their block, forming an invisible barrier that had split them in two before they were old enough to notice. Neither of them had had any say in which school they went to, or who their friends became: everything had been decided for them. This is so often the case with children, and few of them will ever come to resent it, for few of them will ever know.

Every morning the two children got out of bed, put on their clothes, kissed their parents goodbye, and walked away down their ordinary street, through their ordinary town, heading for school in two ordinary, opposite directions. The town where they lived had one extraordinary quality: it was believed to be extraordinarily safe, so that no one thought anything was odd about these children going about their days without an adult to stand close and hold their hands.

Remember this: that it was a very safe, very ordinary town. This will be important later.

The two children were very much alike and very different at the same time, as children so often are. One was named Hepzibah, because her parents had a languid and eccentric way of looking at the world. They called her "Zib," understanding "Hepzibah" was more name than she had shadow. Every day they watched for signs that she was growing into her name, and every day they were disappointed.

"Soon," they promised each other. "Soon."

The other was named Avery, because his parents had a sharp and efficient way of looking at the world. They called him "Avery" when they were happy, and "Avery Alexander Grey" when they were mad, and gave him no nicknames. Nicknames were for people whose names didn't fit them properly, and they had measured him, every inch, before they named him.

"We did well," they reassured each other. "We did."

These are our two children: ordinary, average, wildly unique, as all children are. Mark them well: know them as truly as you know your own hands, your own heartbeat, for they will be the thread we follow through all that is yet to come, and all that has yet to happen.

Our story began on an ordinary, average day, a day which had never happened before and would never, in all the length and breadth of time, happen again. It was a Wednesday, muddled middle of the week, with nothing to recommend it save that when it was over, it would be more than halfway to the weekend. Because Avery and Zib were very much alike, they both enjoyed the weekend, and started looking forward to it when bedtime came calling on Sunday night. Because they were very different, they enjoyed the weekend for very different reasons. Avery liked it because he was allowed to go to the library and sit as long as he liked, reading books that he was still too young to take home with him, but that he was sure would one day teach him all the secrets of the universe. Zib liked it because she was allowed to go to the woods behind her house and play in the little creek that chuckled and tumbled there, catching frogs and staring into their great golden eyes, looking for the answers to questions she hadn't quite figured out yet.

Avery's alarm rang at precisely seven o'clock. He rose from bed without prompting, washed his face and hands and brushed his teeth, and chose his clothing from the selections that had been laid out the night before. He gathered his books and his pencils and his lucky eraser and joined his parents at the breakfast table, where his father spoke of numbers and accounts, and his mother spoke of octaves and arpeggios. His father was a banker, and a very important one at that, managing the money of wealthy people and helping them decide how to make it grow. Avery had planted a nickel once, and it hadn't grown at all, so he suspected that to be a banker was something like being a wizard, only much more powerful.

His mother was a piano teacher, and her lessons were in the very highest demand, for her students were impeccably taught, able to perform under all types of pressure and eagerly sought by symphony orchestras around the country. Had she been a little less in demand, perhaps Avery and Zib would have met years before, for Zib's family fancied themselves musically inclined, and had tried, more than once, to interest her in an instrument. But alas, the lessons given by Avery's mother were always booked years in advance, and no member of Zib's family had ever been that organized.

As for Zib, her alarm didn't go off at all, as she had quite failed to set it the night before, and her parents, being free spirits who believed their daughter should be the same, had chosen not to remind her. She woke at five minutes to eight, gasping in the light, and leapt from her bed without untangling the sheets from around her waist. She grabbed the first clothes she put her hands on, skirt and sweater and mismatched socks, and she ran out the front door without even stopping to say goodbye to her mother, who was sitting at her easel and dreaming of mountains. Zib's father delivered milk to fine houses on the other side of town. He always brought home a pint of cream in the evenings, sweet and fresh and decadent on the tongue. Her mother was a painter, her work in high demand by the very best galleries. Some of Zib's mother's paintings hung in the homes of Avery's father's clients, and none of the parties involved knew how entwined their lives already were.

Now, we have already said that Avery and Zib lived on the same street, and that they were the same age, which means even though they went to different schools, those schools started at the same time. So it was that Zib went rushing out the front door of her house and ran down the sidewalk in one direction as Avery emerged more decorously from his own house and began walking at a brisk pace down the sidewalk in the opposite direction. Neither of them saw the other go.

The doors slammed; their parents did not look up; no one felt that there was anything different, at all, about this day. It was a morning like any other.

It was a morning unlike any other. It was simply that no one had realized it yet.

We must pause for a moment, and consider the shape of the town. Avery and Zib lived on a street that ran along the edge of a forest. Were this a different sort of story, it would be about two children who went camping and got lost, tangled in a wonderland of briars and bears and other terrible things. But this is not that story. Zib knew the woods like they were her own private playground, and would never have become lost there. Avery, on the other hand, would never have willingly set foot in the shadows of the trees, which were tall and terrible and frightening.

The woods stretched on for miles; what was beyond them doesn't matter.

As for the town itself, it was simple and straightforward, designed by clever architects who believed that following rules was the way of the future. They thought there was no need for winding, tree-lined streets or graceful, curving boulevards; everything was set out with precision, all right angles and efficient use of space. They had managed to keep control of the planning office for the better part of twenty years, and under their watchful eyes, every new development and shopping mall had been slotted perfectly into their geometric ideals. A person could walk those streets for years and never once get lost. It was a good place, a safe place, a perfect place to raise a child. That was why, when the doors closed on Avery and Zib's homes, their parents thought nothing of it. Everything was as it should be.

Avery walked with quick, precise steps, content with his place in the world, secure in the knowledge that he knew exactly where he was going and exactly what he was going to find when he got there; he knew the route between home and school better than almost anything, and it held no surprises for him. So it was that when he turned off his street to find his way blocked by construction equipment, he stopped, confused and blinking.

This wasn't supposed to happen. This wasn't in the plan. But the street was broken, cracked like an eggshell, and water gushed up from a hidden, splintered pipe, flooding everything. Men in hard hats swarmed around the break, dropping sandbags and tubes, trying to minimize the damage.

One of them saw Avery and waved. "Sorry, kid," he called. "Water main burst due to an electrical fire. You're going to have to go around."

Avery's mouth worked, but no sound came out. Go around? Go *around*? He had walked the same path to school every day since he'd been old enough to start going to school at all. His parents trusted him to walk *this* way, to follow the clear and sensible rules that were there to keep him safe. He had never considered going a different way. He didn't know how.

The man in the hard hat, for all that he is a minor character in this story, as so many people must be—for a story is, by its very nature, a narrow thing, focused on *this* hero and *this* villain, on making them the most important people in the world, and hence excluding anyone who might be a threat to their positions—offered the boy a sympathetic smile. "It'll be fine," he said. "All you need to do is go up the block to the next street and you can get around the damage."

Avery disagreed. Everything was *not* fine. But he had been raised to listen when adults spoke, and so he merely nodded, tightened his hand on the strap holding his books in place, and turned to go back the way he'd come.

As for Zib, she walked along the perfectly straight sidewalk in a wavy, erratic line, sometimes slowing to a crawl to watch a snail working its way down the pavement, sometimes running to make up the time she'd spent malingering. "Malingering" was one of her favorite words. Her teachers liked to use it about her when they thought she wasn't listening—which, to be fair, was always. Zib had a way of making people think she was paying attention to anything but them, when in fact, she was taking careful note of everything that happened around her.

When she reached the end of the block, she turned and stopped, cocking her head to the side as she solemnly, silently considered the scene in front of her. She had walked this way just the day before, twice, once coming and once going, and she was quite sure that there had been a street there. A *whole* street, not just two pieces framing a pit that went down, down, down into the depths of the town's foundations. Workers in hard hats swarmed around the hole, putting up barriers and taking measurements, too distracted to have noticed her yet.

It must have only just happened, she thought; there would have been sirens otherwise, big and loud and clanging. Her mother would have come out to see what all the fuss was about, and then she would have called the school to say that Zib wasn't coming in, and it would have been pancakes and finger paints and a day spent happily at home.

But it would also have been missing math class, and Zib thought that math might be the best thing that anyone had ever invented; the rest of school was worth suffering through if at the end of it she got to see the way the numbers danced. She took a cautious step forward.

A woman in an orange safety vest paused in the process of setting another caution sign near the edge of the hole and called, "Hey! You can't be here!"

Zib, who was very much present, stopped and blinked at her. Adults were always saying things like that. "You can't be here" didn't change the fact that "here" was a place, and Zib was already *in* the place, making the statement nonsensical at best, and false at worst.

"Look, kiddo, a gas line blew, and the whole street's closed. Are you trying to get to school?"

Zib nodded.

"You're going to have to go around."

Zib frowned and pointed to the intact sidewalk.

The woman shook her head. "It's not safe. I'm sorry. If you back up and try the next street, you should be fine. You won't even be late for school."

Adults were always so sure of things like that, and there was no sense in arguing with them: once they decided that something was so, they would argue and yell and send children to their rooms to get their way. Zib wasn't entirely sure why being old made you right, but it definitely made you bigger, and she didn't want to fight with someone who was bigger than she was. So she shrugged, and turned, and went back the way she had come.

Because their houses, Avery's and Zib's both, were on the side of the street where the forest loomed, there were no corners: they lived, unwittingly, only three doors down from one another. But across the street from them was another road, right between the one where Avery walked to school and the one where Zib walked to school. They approached it, Avery walking with quick, precise steps, Zib skipping and strolling and sometimes outright running, and they reached their respective corners at the same time.

It would seem reasonable for them to have seen each other, for them to have noticed each other, for something to have begun with two children on two corners on an ordinary day that was quickly going wrong. But Avery was thinking about the water and the way it had filled the street, and Zib was thinking about the hole and the way it had seemed to go on forever, and so they both turned without looking to see who might be watching, and they walked down the road, one on either side, both of them thinking they were entirely alone.

Everything that had happened so far, from alarm clocks ringing or not ringing to breakfasts being eaten or not eaten to holes opening in streets where holes had never been before . . . everything that had happened had been something entirely possible, if not entirely probable. The world is divided, after all, into possible and impossible, and something which is possible can happen whenever it sees fit, even if it is inconvenient or unwanted. Something which is *im*possible, however, is never supposed to happen at all, and when it does—for it would be impossible for the impossible to go away entirely—it tends to disrupt things rather conclusively.

So it was, perhaps, more reasonable than it seemed for Avery and Zib, upon reaching the end of the block, to find themselves looking, not at another block like the last, but at a wall only slightly higher than Zib was tall, made of large, rough-hewn bricks. Avery, who was a few inches shorter than she, but who knew something about rocks, thought they might be granite. Zib, who had never been very interested in rocks when not skipping them across the surface of a pond, thought the flowering moss growing between the bricks might be the sort of thing lizards liked to use for a mattress. Both of them thought the wall had no business being there.

The wall, which did not care what anyone thought of it, continued to exist.

It was a very pretty wall, well crafted and sturdy. Avery's parents would have approved of the craftsmanship. Zib's parents would have approved of the wildflowers that grew along its base and the lichen that grew along its top. It looked weathered and wise and oddly permanent, like it would still be there long after the rest of the town had been forgotten.

Avery gaped at the wall. He didn't have the words for what he felt as he looked at it. There wasn't a wall here. He had been down this street a hundred times, walking with his parents or sitting in the backseat of their car, and there had never *been* a wall here, certainly not one that looked older than any of the houses around it.

If Avery had been able to ask an adult what he was feeling, they would have given him a word: offense. The wall was an offense. It was an impossible thing in a possible place, and it should never have been allowed, not for a moment, not ever. It hurt him to look at it, like it was there only to mock him.

Zib grinned at the wall. Her feelings were no less complicated than Avery's, but they were more familiar to her, because she had been feeling them almost every day she could remember. She felt delight, yes, and excitement, and a small measure of what she would have refused to identify as relief if anyone had asked her. Not being willing to name a thing doesn't change what it *is*, however, and Zib was relieved.

This was something new. This was something different. This might mean missing math class, and she would be sad about that later, but right here, right now, this was an *adventure*.

Adventures do not come along every day, or every week, or even every year. Adventures are shy, unpredictable things, and they swoop in when least expected, carrying their victims away from their average, everyday worlds and into something marvelous. Zib had been waiting *so* long for something marvelous to come for her. She was the first of them to approach the wall, touching the rough stones with one shaking hand, grin growing even wider when she confirmed that yes, *yes*, it was real; this was happening.

Dropping her half-eaten apple to the ground, she grasped the highest brick she could reach and began pulling herself up, scrabbling until she was sure she had her balance. Once she was high enough, she slung one leg over the top of the wall, pausing to catch her breath and look back.

We will return to her in a moment. Let us look, briefly, to Avery, who stood looking at the wall with wide, offended eyes, waiting for it to go away. It did not go away. He reached out and touched it, snatching his fingers away as if they had been burned by the brief contact, and still it did not go away, and still it was between him and the school.

If a wall where a wall was not meant to be was an offense, that same wall keeping him from making it to class on time was unthinkable. Avery looked in one direction and then the other, trying to find a way around the wall. There was none. It extended the width of the street, and across the yards of the houses to either side, stopping only when it reached their windows and could go no further. The only way forward was over.

Slower than Zib, more hesitantly, Avery began to climb.

When he reached the top, he looked back, not realizing that a girl he had never met before was doing the same thing in the very same instant. Together, they gazed down what should have been a street they both knew well, toward the place where their homes should have been.

There was nothing there but forest.

The houses were gone. The telephone posts and streetlights and lawns were gone. Even the street, where they had been standing only moments before, was gone, replaced by tree roots and broken ground and trailing ferns. Zib made a strangled squawking noise and fell, landing on the far side of the wall. Avery continued to stare, his shoulders shaking as he tried to deny the change. Then, with the calm precision of a boy who didn't know what else to do, he swung his legs over the wall's edge. Once he was on the other side, everything would return to normal. It would have to.

The wind blew down an empty street, where there were no children with hair to be ruffled or jackets to be flapped, and where there was no wall to stop or slow it, and everything was ordinary, and nothing was ordinary at all.

TWO

OVER THE WOODWARD WALL

Zib stared up at the sky, her head still spinning with the impossibility of what she had just seen. Her house, gone. Her mother, gone. All her toys and clothes and books and games, gone. She knew, in a distant way, that not all those things were equal—that some of them should have been more upsetting than others—but they were all so big and so impossible that she couldn't start untangling them from one another.

She would have to figure things out as she went along. She sat up, and discovered that her fall had been broken by a cluster of ferns the likes of which she had never seen before. Their fronds were proper fern-fronds, long and curling and almost mathematical in their perfection, but each one of them was a different shade of blue, from the color of the sky at midnight to the color of a robin's egg in the morning. She had never seen blue ferns before, and she unsnarled herself from them carefully, afraid of hurting them.

Avery, who had climbed down more cautiously, turned in a slow circle as he tried to decide what was happening. There was no street on this side of the wall. There were no houses. There was only forest, vast and wild and tangled in a way that the woods behind his house had never been. The woods weren't his playground the way they were Zib's, but they weren't like this. This was . . . old, somehow, old and strange and not unwelcoming, exactly, but not happy to see him, either.

Zib, shaking the last bit of fern off her shoe, cleared her throat. "Um," she said. "Hello."

It was not the most remarkable introduction as such things go. It would, however, have to do. Avery turned, and the two of them saw each other for the first time. Avery looked at Zib, and Zib looked at Avery, and neither of them knew quite what to do with what they saw.

Avery saw a girl his age, in a sweater that was too big for her and a skirt with mended tears all the way around the hem. Some of them were sewn better than others. Some of them were on the verge of ripping open again. Her socks were mismatched and her sweater was patched, and her hair was so wild that if she had reached into it and produced a full set of silverware, a cheese sandwich, and a live frog, he would not have been surprised. She had mud under her nails and scabs on her knees, and was not at all the sort of person his parents liked him to associate with.

Zib saw a boy her age, in a shirt that was too white and pants that were too pressed. Her reflection stared back at her from the surface of his polished shoes, wide-eyed and goggling. His cuffs were buttoned and his jacket was pristine, making him look like a very small mortician who had somehow wandered into the wrong sort of neighborhood, one where there were too many living people and not nearly enough dead ones. He had carefully clipped nails and looked like he had never ridden a bike in his life, and was not at all the sort of person her parents liked her to associate with.

"What are *you* doing here?" they asked in unison, and stopped, and stared at each other, and said nothing further. They were standing in the middle of a mystery. Mysteries needed to be explored.

Zib turned to look at the wall. It was still there, which was almost surprising, given how many other things had disappeared. She reached out and tapped it. It felt solid, like stone was supposed to feel. The moss felt cool and fuzzy, like velvet. Every sense she had told her that the wall was real, real, *real*. But when she started to reach for a handhold, she stopped, suddenly overcome with the absolute conviction that climbing back was not the answer.

Avery was not so calm. He gaped at the blue ferns, and then at the trees, which had leaves as clear as glass, as thin as the pages of a book. "Trees can't photosynthesize without chlorophyll," he said. "They'd starve and die if they tried. These trees aren't real. These trees can't be real."

"The wall's real," said Zib.

"I said the *trees* weren't real."

"The trees look pretty real to me." Zib tapped the wall again before turning abruptly to Avery. "I have a dime and three acorns and a seashell my uncle gave me for luck, and you can have them all if you'll climb back over the wall."

Avery paused. "What?"

"They're all in my pocket. See?" She stuck her hand into the rough pocket sewn to the front of her skirt and pulled out her treasures, holding them out toward him. "You can have them. But you have to climb the wall."

"Why . . . wait." Avery's eyes narrowed in sudden suspicion. "Why don't *you* climb the wall?"

Zib hesitated before putting her hand back in her pocket, tucking her treasures away. "I don't think it's real. I think the trees are real and the wall isn't."

"But that doesn't make any sense at all! We just came from the other side of the wall. If it wasn't real, we couldn't have climbed over it."

"So climb it," said Zib stubbornly. "Climb it and prove me wrong, why don't you?"

"Maybe I will!" Avery turned to face the wall. His anger collapsed in his chest, replaced by a hollow place that felt a little bit like fear and a little bit like wariness and a lot like wishing his alarm clock hadn't rung at all but had left him to sleep in and need his father to give him a ride to school. He usually hated those days. Right now, he would have welcomed it.

The wall didn't look exactly like it had looked before he had climbed over it: no two sides of the same thing ever look *exactly* alike. But the stones looked like they could be the same stones, viewed from behind, and the moss and lichen looked like they could be the same kind of moss and lichen, and who was this girl, anyway, to tell him what to do, to bribe him with trash and pretend that it was treasure? All he had to do was climb and she would know that he was brave, and clever, and *right*.

All he had to do was climb and they would both know that walls didn't disappear just because someone crossed them. Maybe the forest would feel ashamed of being here when it wasn't supposed to, and fade away, letting the streets and houses and ordinary things come back. He tried to hold that thought in the front of his mind. If he went back over the wall, everything would be normal again.

He reached out. He touched the stone. For a moment—just a moment—it was cool and solid and faintly rough, the way real bricks always were.

Then, without warning, it was gone. Avery stumbled forward, into the cloud shaped like a wall, and watched in horror as it broke apart and drifted away, popping like a soap bubble in the morning air. There wasn't even a line of empty earth to show where it had been, no, there were ferns and flowers and rocks and bushes and if someone had told him that there had never been a wall at all, he would have had trouble arguing, because the evidence of his eyes was so very, very clear.

Avery put his hands against the sides of his face and

stared at the place where the wall belonged. The wall did not return.

"Guess you don't get my seashell," said Zib thoughtfully. She wiped her hand against her skirt and stuck it out toward him. "I'm Zib."

"That's not a name," Avery mumbled.

"It is *so*," she protested. "It's *my* name, and it's what my parents call me, and that means it's as good and real as any other name. It's short for 'Hepzibah.'"

Avery turned to look at her, hands still pressed against his face. "So your name is Hepzibah."

"No. That's my name for when I'm older." Zib had a vague sense that Hepzibah would always wear socks that matched, would never tear her skirts or dirty her blouses or climb trees just to see whether the squirrels had anything interesting tucked away in their nests. Hepzibah would probably like all her classes, not just math, and her parents would love her more than they had ever loved silly, grubby Zib.

Zib didn't like Hepzibah very much. They might share a skeleton, but they would never share a skin.

"Names don't work like that," protested Avery. "My name is Avery. It's Avery now, and it's Avery tomorrow, and it was Avery yesterday. Once you have a name, it's yours. You can't just slice it up and use the parts you like."

"Can so!"

"Can not!"

"Can *so*!"

A shadow passed over them, huge and dark and silent. The children froze, looking slowly skyward. There was nothing there. A nearby tree creaked ominously. They looked down.

The owl that had landed on a branch almost even with their eyes looked back at them. A birdwatcher would have gasped at the sight, fumbling for their binoculars and bird book, intent on recording this remarkable moment. Avery and Zib simply stared. Avery, who had watched a great many nature shows despite not liking the outdoors, thought that it might be the biggest owl in the entire world. It was easily as tall as he was, with tufted feathers forming "ears" on the sides of its head that made it look even taller. Zib, who knew all the owls living in the woods behind her house, thought she had never seen a blue owl before. It was as blue as the ferns, banded in midnight and morning, with a belly the color of the ceaseless sea.

The owl looked at Avery and Zib. Avery and Zib looked at the owl. It was difficult not to notice how long the owl's talons were, or how sharp its beak was, or how wide and orange its eyes were. Looking directly at them was like trying to have a staring contest with the whole of Halloween.

Privately, Avery guessed that the owl did not give away licorice or candy apples on Halloween night. Dead stoats and stitches were much more likely.

"You are very loud," said the owl finally. "If you must spend the whole day fighting, could you do it under someone else's tree?" The owl had a soft and pleasant voice, like a nanny, and while there was a slight lisp to its words, both Avery and Zib could understand it perfectly. They blinked in unison, bemused.

"I didn't know owls could talk," said Zib.

"Of course owls can talk," said the owl. "Everything can talk. It's simply a matter of learning how best to listen."

"No," said Avery.

Zib and the owl turned to look at him. He shook his head.

"No," he repeated, and "*No,*" he said a third time, for emphasis. "I'm supposed to be going to school. I should be *at* school by now, not standing here arguing with an owl next to a wall that isn't there."

"You're right about one thing," said the owl. "There isn't a wall there at all. I don't know all the names you humans use for the things you build, but I know what a wall is, and I know what a wall isn't, and unless humans have started building invisible walls, that isn't one." The owl blinked. As its eyes were very large, this took quite some time. "Humans *haven't* started building invisible walls, have they? Because that would be very unneighborly of you. Glass is bad enough. Invisible walls would be a step too far."

"Can you be next to something that isn't there?" asked Zib.

Avery glared at them both. "Don't make fun of me," he said.

"I'm not," protested Zib. "I asked because I really want to know!"

The owl heaved a heavy sigh. "You're children, aren't you?"

"Yes," said Zib. "Can't you tell?"

"Humans always look the same to me once they're old enough to leave the nest. Hatchling humans are one thing, but the rest of you? Pssh." The owl waved a wing. "All gangly and flightless and odd. It's no wonder you cover yourselves with artificial feathers. I wouldn't want to go around looking plucked all the time either, if I were you. But the two of you, you squawk and flail your flightless little wings, and those things usually mean 'child' when it's humans involved. What are you doing here?"

"We climbed over the wall that isn't there," said Avery. "Where are we?"

"Well, you're in the Forest of Borders," said the owl. "The forest is very large, so that may not help you as much as you would like it to, but it's where you are, and it's where you'll be until you decide to let your feet take you someplace else. You're under my tree, which is more specific but even less helpful, since it doesn't tell you where anything else is. Where are your nests?"

"On the other side of the wall," said Avery miserably.

Unlike Zib, he had never gone wishing for adventures, and had always thought that he wouldn't know what to do with one if it happened to come along. Now that he was being proven right, he found that he didn't enjoy it in the least. This wasn't the sort of right answer that was rewarded with hot chocolate and fresh cookies and pats on the head; this was the sort of right answer that came after a question like "Do you think it will hurt?" or "Do you know whose turn it is to do the dishes?"

For perhaps the first time in his life, Avery found himself wishing he'd been wrong.

"Ah," said the owl, understanding. "Poor children. You didn't know you were on a border, did you? And when you're on a border, if you step wrong, you can find yourself in the forest."

"Can we step back?" asked Zib.

"No, I'm afraid not. You're not on a border anymore, you see; you're someplace. The only way to get back to where you were is to find another border, one that crosses in the opposite direction."

"You said this was the Forest of Borders," said Avery. "Shouldn't we be able to find a border here?"

"Good gracious, no," said the owl. "This isn't the Forest of Border *Crossings,* or the Forest of Getting Where You Need to Go."

"Do those places exist?" asked Avery.

"If they do, I've never been there," said the owl. "This is the Forest of Borders. When you step over a border without a destination in mind, you wind up here, at least until you go somewhere else. Where were you trying to go?"

Avery and Zib exchanged a look.

"To school," said Avery.

"On an adventure," said Zib.

"One of you might get your way, but I can't say which one," said the owl. "Maybe both of you will, and won't that be an interesting thing to watch? My name is Meadowsweet. Do you have names?"

"Avery," said Avery.

"Zib," said Zib.

"You shouldn't lie to talking owls," said Avery. "That's not your name."

Zib glared at him. "It is so."

"No, it's not," said Avery. "Your name is Hepzibah."

"A piece can represent the whole," said Meadowsweet. "If the human child wants to hold up a branch and say it means the entire tree, I don't see where it's another human child's place to stop it. Representative symbols are an essential piece of making so many things. Without them, we wouldn't have maps, or books, or paintings. Peace, human child. Let your fellow be."

Avery crossed his arms, chin dropping in a sulk, while Zib beamed.

"Now, then, we have more important matters to discuss, like getting you out of the forest and away from my tree."

"Why?" asked Zib. "Are we not allowed to be here?"

"You're allowed to be wherever you are, and I'm quite sure I don't set the rules for either one of you, but there are consequences to being in places, and one of the consequences of being in the forest is you making noise under my tree and keeping me awake." Meadowsweet puffed up, feathers standing on end, until the outline became less "owl" and more "dandelion going to seed." "I would prefer to sleep, so you must go."

"That doesn't seem fair," said Avery.

"Also, there is the small matter of you being eaten by wolves if you stay here, flightless creatures that you are."

"Oh," said Avery, more subdued. "How do we get out of the forest?"

The owl, who was kinder than she sounded—who had raised three nests of eggs to adulthood, and most of them owls in their own right, with the occasional gryphon and harpy thrown in to keep her on her talons—took pity. She launched herself from her branch, wings spread wide, and glided down to land in front of the children. "Do you have anything of use with you?"

"I have a slingshot and some rocks," said Zib. "And I have my math homework and a sandwich and an apple."

"I have my books, and I have the metal ruler I won last year in the spelling bee," said Avery. He had never been able to quite understand why the reward for being the best at spelling was a ruler, which didn't know how to spell anything, but it had been so nice to win a prize that he had never wanted to argue.

"It's a start," said Meadowsweet. She turned to Zib. "A slingshot—that's the human weapon that throws things away from itself, very fast, isn't it?"

"It's a toy, not a weapon," said Zib. "But yes."

"I suppose whether it's a toy or a weapon depends on whether you're aiming it or having it aimed at you," said Meadowsweet. "Take a rock, and put it in your slingshot, and throw the rock as far as the slingshot will let you. Once you've done that, go looking for it. Three rocks should see you to the end of the forest. Maybe five. Definitely not four. Four is an even number, and those never get you anywhere."

"Will you come with us?" asked Avery. Meadow-sweet was an owl, which was strange, but she was also an adult. Things always went more smoothly when there was an adult around.

To his surprise, the owl laughed. "Me, go with you? You're human children, and clearly on a quest for something, even if it's only the wall you say you've misplaced. I value my wings too much to accompany human children on a quest. Only head for the edge of the forest, and you'll find something there to help you."

"How can you be so sure?" asked Zib.

"Things have a way of going the way they're meant to go. You should start walking. The wolves will be here soon." Meadowsweet took off in a flurry of wings, vanishing back into the high branches, and for all that she was impossibly blue, no matter how much Zib and Avery squinted, they couldn't see her.

"Now what do we do?" asked Avery.

Zib slid her hands into two of the pockets hidden in her skirt, coming up with a slingshot and a polished stone the size of a conker. She pulled the strap on her slingshot back, slid the stone into the cup at the center of the strap, and let go, sending the stone sailing straight and true through the trees.

"We go that way," she said, and started walking.

Avery stayed where he was, staring after her. Zib kept going for a few more feet before pausing and look-ing back.

"Well?" she asked. "Are you coming?"

Avery scrambled to catch up with her, and the two children walked into the trees, not quite together but not quite alone, following the trail of the slingshot stone.

THREE

THE IMPROBABLE ROAD

Meadowsweet's directions had not been very precise, not when compared to a lifetime of hearing things like "turn left on Main" or "three doors down, you can't miss it." Following a small stone through a tangled forest was difficult, and strange, and sometimes unpredictable. The slingshot was strong enough to throw the stones quite far, and Zib's aim was good, but she wasn't aiming *at* anything, only trying to send the stones away from the two of them with all the force she could. Finding the stones after they landed was hard.

But after they found the first one, the trees got a little less foreboding. After they found the second one, the shadows got a little shallower, like the sun had remembered it had a job to do. And when Zib reached under a fern the color of strawberry taffy to retrieve the third stone, she heard Avery gasp.

"I can see a road!" he shouted.

She looked up to see him running through the trees, stumbling over roots and slapping branches aside in his haste to get out of the forest. Fear washed through her, sharp and biting. He was going to leave her behind. He was going to leave her all alone in this unfamiliar place, and she was going to be eaten by wolves. She didn't know him very well—didn't really know him at all, except that his cuffs were too tight and he didn't like adventures— but she didn't like the idea of being all alone. No, she didn't like that one bit.

"Wait for me!" She shoved slingshot and stone both into the pocket of her skirt and took off after him.

The edge of a forest is something entirely different from the heart of a forest, which only makes sense, really: an edge is a beginning, or an ending, and not a comfortable middle. Perhaps that was why Avery froze as soon as he was out of the shadow of the trees, shaking slightly, like an arrow on the verge of being released from a bow. Zib stopped next to him, raking twigs out of the wild tangle of her hair, and followed his gaze. She blinked, slowly.

There was a road. There was nothing else it could have been: she knew no other name for a ribbon of brick winding its way through a valley, surrounded by grassy, flower-covered hills, bridging narrow streams. But where most of the bricks she had seen were red, or gray, or a dull, disappointing brown, this road gleamed with iridescent rainbows, like every brick had been coated in a thin layer of mother-of-pearl. It was beautiful. It looked fragile, and impractical, and—

"Impossible," said Avery, and his voice was brown-brick dull. It was the voice of a boy on the very verge of giving up. "This can't be happening. It can't be *real*. I'm asleep, I have to be." He turned to Zib, suddenly frantic as he grabbed at her hands. "Slap me. I need you to slap me as hard as you can, so I'll wake up."

"What happens to me if you wake up?" demanded Zib, and took a big step back, away from his snatching fingers. "I don't think I'm dreaming. But if you're dreaming, and you wake up, do I pop like a soap bubble? I don't want to pop. I'm finally having an adventure."

"This isn't an adventure!" shouted Avery.

A new voice rang out. "Ah, but are you sure that you're the one who gets to decide that?"

The two children turned, Zib moving a little closer to Avery.

At first, it seemed they were alone on the shallow, grassy hill that descended from forest to road. The trees were there, and whatever lived among the trees—Meadowsweet, certainly, and wolves, perhaps, and all manner of other things—but trees weren't good company, and the things that lived in them weren't showing themselves.

There was a boulder off to one side, large and rough and glittering in the sun, veined in pink and black and creamy white, like a scoop of harlequin ice cream. It shivered, which was not a thing boulders were much known to do. It shuddered, which was also not a thing boulders were much known to do. Finally, it unfolded itself, like a piece of paper being smoothed out on a table to show the hidden picture inside, and became a man.

He was not a very tall man, being scarcely taller than Avery himself, and he was not a very fat man, as Zib could easily have linked a single arm around his waist, but he was a very handsome man, with sculpted features under a fringe of black-pink-white hair, and a smart suit that seemed to have been tailored from the stone that comprised his body. He looked at the children with interest.

"You're not from around here, and if you're not from around here, you must have come from somewhere else, and if you've come from somewhere else, you're almost certainly having an adventure," said the man. "I'm sorry to be the one to tell you that, if you didn't *want* an adventure, but sometimes adventures happen whether or not they're requested. They're like Tuesday afternoons, or headaches, or birthdays. They do as they like."

"You were a boulder," accused Zib. "Boulders can't talk."

"This can't be happening, boulders can't talk—tell me, does *anything* happen where you come from?" The man looked at them with unalloyed concern. "It sounds very dull."

"Who are you?" asked Avery.

"My name is Quartz," said the man. "As to who I am, that is an existential question. 'Existential' means 'pertaining to existence,' which I suppose means that asking for a cookie is existential, which means it's a word with no useful applications, and you should forget you know it."

"We know the word 'existential,'" said Avery. "We're not *babies*."

"Ah, but here, at least, you *are* babes in the woods, or babes out of the woods, as it happens, and you don't think boulders can talk and you don't think adventures can do as they like, and I think that means you need a guide." Quartz removed his hat and bowed, deeply. "At your service, for as long as the improbable road will keep us together."

"The what?" asked Zib.

"The improbable road. I don't mean to insult you, but do you know what 'improbable' means?"

"Unlikely," said Avery.

"Is it unlikely that you know, or does the word mean 'unlikely'? As it happens, both are true, so we'll carry merrily on, or we could be here playing dictionary all night, and that doesn't get us anywhere. Literally. We won't move." Quartz replaced his hat atop his head before indicating the road with a sweep of one hand. "Bricks made from sunlight on sand and moonlight on mist and starlight on water? Improbable! A single road that runs the length of an entire kingdom? Improbable! A city of untold marvels and incredible wonders waiting at its end? Improbable! So this, then, must be the improbable road, and if you walk it long enough, all your questions will be answered, for what could be more improbable than a happy ending? Of course, for you to make it without a guide would be . . ." He paused portentously.

Zib, feeling quite sure of herself, chirped, "Improbable!"

"Oh, no, child, no," said Quartz. "For you to make it without a guide would be *impossible,* which is something entirely different, and far less pleasant."

"There's a city?" asked Avery. "Can we go there?" Cities meant adults, and policemen, and other people who could make things start making sense again.

"If you want to get anything done, you'll *have* to go there," said Quartz. "The Impossible City is where things finish."

"You mean where things begin," said Avery.

"If I'd meant that, I would have said that," said Quartz. "What is a conversation like where you come from, if no one ever says the things they mean to be saying? You've already begun, unless a beginning is something different when you're at home: see, you're standing here, talking with me, outside the Forest of Borders, and the only way to enter the forest is to cross a border. The improbable road is right there waiting for you, ready to sweep you away to the next stage of the adventure you don't want to have. No, the beginning is well behind us now. It's the ending you need to move toward."

"What do we have to do?" asked Zib, who was getting the distinct feeling that if she allowed Avery to make the decisions, they would be standing there until well after the sun went down, assuming such silly things as "sunsets" existed in a world of talking owls and helpful boulders.

"You have to walk the length of the improbable road, all the way to the Impossible City, where—if you've been clever, and you've been cunning, and most of all, if you've been correct—the Queen of Wands will see that you've earned an ending, and send you back to wherever you've come from, or wherever you want to be, which isn't necessarily, or even often, the same thing."

"The Queen of what?" asked Zib.

"The Queen of Wands. She's the best and brightest of the four rulers of the Up-and-Under. She burns so bright, it's like sitting in the presence of a star." Quartz smiled, a dreamy look in his eyes. "I should be in the service of the King of Coins, what with him being in charge of the earth and all the things that grow there, but I've always been more inclined to glitter when I can, not sit about being stolid and dependable. It's the Queen of Wands for me. She's in the Impossible City right now. She has been for years upon years upon years, and she'll help you if you get there."

"Wait," said Avery. "We don't have a Queen. We certainly don't have four of them."

"We don't have four queens either," said Quartz. "We have two, one you'd like to meet and one you wouldn't, and two kings, who keep to themselves, except when they don't, and who needn't be involved with this at all. The Queen of Wands will help you, you'll see. She's the best of them."

Zib, who was not always as quick as Avery to realize when something was wrong, frowned. "What's the Up-and-Under?" she asked.

"This is!" Quartz spread his arms, indicating the forest, the hills, the winding, iridescent road. "All of this is the Up-and-Under, and a great deal more than this. It exists even when people aren't looking, which you must agree is a desirable quality in a world, and so there are oceans and mountains and bakeries where the bread is very good and bakeries where the bread is very bad and cheesemakers and cats and *everything*. Oh! But you must come from another kind of kingdom, if you don't know these things."

"We don't come from a kingdom at all," said Avery. "We come from a country called the United States of America. We stopped having kings and queens years and years ago. We have a President instead, and he does what's right for the country, not what's right for the crown."

"What happens if your Resident decides that what's right for the country isn't what everyone else thinks is right?" asked Quartz, with the sort of polite puzzlement that adults always seemed to bring to games of make-believe.

Avery rankled. "We have elections, and we elect

someone else to be *President*." He tried to make the "P" as loud as possible, so that the crystal man would hear it.

"What a funny way of doing things," said Quartz. "Here, if one of the kings or queens gets too big for their britches, we just march on the Impossible City with pitchforks and spears and very large spiders, and we boot out whomever's in ascension and replace them with someone who will do a better job."

"That sounds like an election," said Zib dubiously.

"Oh, no, it isn't elective at all. When someone with a very large spider asks you to move along, you move."

Zib glanced anxiously at the forest's edge. All this talk of very large spiders had her worried that some of them might show up to ask for a place in the story. She wasn't *afraid* of spiders, exactly. Being afraid of spiders was a silly, squeamish thing, and she hated being silly, and she hated being squeamish. She simply thought that spiders were best when viewed from a distance. The greater the distance, the better.

"Is the Queen of Wands really waiting for us?" she asked.

"She is, she is, and she's a very busy woman; you had best get moving, if you want to catch her before she gets tired of waiting and decides to do something else." Quartz gestured toward the shining road. "Your ending lies ahead."

Avery looked at Zib. Zib looked at Avery. Avery looked at the sky, which was wide and blue and some-how subtly wrong, like the shapes of the clouds weren't what they ought to be, like the birds that soared on distant winds would, if they came closer, be revealed as dragons, or winged horses, or winged *people*. Zib looked at the forest, which was welcoming and foreboding at the same time, filled with ferns that were the wrong colors and trees that had the wrong leaves. Both of them looked at the road.

"We just . . . walk?" asked Avery. "That's all?"

"You walk *improbably*," said Quartz. "And here is where I give you a word of caution, although I'm sure you don't need it, clever children that you are. You began this story together, whether you intended to or not. You'll end it the same way, or you won't end it at all."

"What does that mean?" asked Zib.

"It means we both go home or neither of us does," said Avery.

Quartz tapped the side of his nose with one striated finger. "Clever boy, yes, indeed! All or nothing, that's the way in the Impossible City. All or nothing."

Avery and Zib exchanged another look.

They wouldn't be able to explain why later, if anyone asked them at all, but they started walking at the same time, and when they reached the road, they kept on walking, with Quartz walking alongside them, still disconcertingly made of crystal.

They had been walking for some time—long enough for Zib to have climbed and fallen out of three different trees growing alongside the road—when Quartz waved them to a halt. The crystal man's formerly jocular face was set into a scowl.

"What," he asked, "do you think you're doing?"

"We're walking to the Impossible City so the Queen of Wands will give us an ending and send us home," said Avery, and frowned, because that sentence should have made no sense at all.

"No, you're not," said Quartz. "To get to the Impossible City, you need to walk the improbable road."

"But we are!" protested Zib.

"You're *not*," said Quartz. "Everything you've done has been completely plain and probable. If you want to walk the improbable road, you need to find it."

Avery and Zib exchanged a look. This was going to be more difficult than they had expected.

"How can you be improbable on purpose?" asked Avery.

"I don't know," said Quartz.

Zib frowned. Zib sat down in the middle of the road and began picking at her hair, dislodging leaves and twigs and a small, startled lizard that had been there since she'd fallen out of the first tree.

"Get up," said Avery. "We have to keep walking."

"No," said Zib. "I don't think we do."

"What do you mean?"

Zib got back to her feet. "I think it's probable that if you follow a road, you'll wind up going where the road goes. So that means that if you *don't* follow the road, it's *improbable* that you'll wind up going where the road goes. So *that* means that if we want to follow the improbable road, we can't follow it at all. Come on, Avery!"

She grabbed the boy's hand and broke into a run,

dragging him off the road and into the meadow on the other side. A wall of thorns burst from the ground behind them, cutting them off from Quartz and from the road.

Quartz smiled.

"Well," he said. "That took them long enough." Whistling, he began strolling onward, toward the distant, unseen spires of the Impossible City.

FOUR

THE CROW GIRL

Avery was not very fond of running. They did running three times a week at school, and he was always one of the very slowest, circling the track behind the rest of his class, lungs burning and legs aching and shoes pinching his feet. All those things happened now, as he ran with Zib. His breath whistled in his throat, which seemed to have gotten somehow smaller, forgetting what it was supposed to do. His legs were too long and too short at the same time, and his shoes hurt his feet, making him utterly aware of every single toe.

And he was laughing.

It seemed strange that he should laugh while he was being dragged across a meadow by a girl he'd only barely met and who wasn't at all the sort of friend he was invited to bring home for lemonade and cookies.

His mother would have sniffed at Zib's hair, and his father would have scowled at Zib's clothes, but here they were together, having an adventure, and he knew, deep down, that as long as she held on to his hand, he would be just fine.

He was still marveling over this impossible truth when his foot hit a stone and he went sprawling, his hand yanked from Zib's by gravity. The grass, which had seemed dry when they were running across it, had pulled the trick beloved of grasses everywhere and hidden its wetness away down among its roots: as soon as Avery fell, he began to slide, slowly at first, then with growing speed, as his weight pressed the wetness out of the grass and into the soil beneath him.

The mud was candy-striped, pink and blue and purple, streaked with veins of golden glitter. Avery was too busy shrieking to appreciate it.

"Avery!"

Zib had been happy running through the meadow with her strange new friend beside her. Unlike Avery, she had always seen the value in being able to run faster than anyone expected, and she had been so delighted with her own cleverness that it had never occurred to her that he might feel differently. Now, watching him wheeze and yell as a sudden cascade of colorful mud carried him away, she wondered whether it might not have been a good idea to go a little slower.

There was a plopping, cascading sound. Zib ran along the stream of mud, which was swelling so that she thought soon it might be better to call it a river, and stared in horror as she saw what was happening: the mud was pouring over a cliff, and soon, Avery would pour over the cliff too.

"Avery, swim!"

Avery stopped thrashing as he turned and gave her a wide-eyed, open-mouthed look. "It's *mud*!"

"I noticed!"

"I can't swim in mud!"

"Why not? Try!" The cliff was getting closer. Zib couldn't decide whether telling him would be a good thing—a motivation—or a bad thing, since no one really likes to hear that they're about to be swept over a cliff and maybe drowned in mud.

Avery, to his credit, tried. He kicked his legs and flailed his arms, and all he managed to do was go under the mud, disappearing for one heart-stopping moment before he bobbed back to the surface, choking and coughing, with blue and purple streaks on his face. "I can't!" he wailed.

Zib ran alongside the river of mud—when had it become wide enough for her to think of it as a river? This wasn't improbable, this was *impossible,* and her heart rebelled from it even as her mind began looking for ways to make it go away—and considered her options as quickly as she could. If she dove in, they could both be swept over the cliff. She didn't know Avery very well. Maybe she could find the Impossible City without him. The mud looked soft; he would probably be fine.

But then she would always, forever, be the kind of person who didn't dive in when she saw that a friend who had made a little, simple mistake was being swept away by consequences he could never have predicted. She would walk in the shadow of that decision for the rest of her life. She would see that person in the mirror.

Zib took a deep breath, kicked off her shoes, which had never fit that well in the first place, and threw herself into the river of mud.

Avery had been right about one thing: it was difficult to swim in the mud. Zib, who had spent substantially more time in mudholes and ditches than he had, thought there was something strange about that; normally, moving through mud was a little difficult but not altogether impossible. *This* mud was almost like thin taffy. It grabbed at her arms and legs, pulling them down, keeping her from getting any sort of traction. She fought against it all the same, and reached Avery, grabbing hold of his wrist, barely a second before the river of mud carried them both over the cliff.

The mud roared as it slid around them. The mud thundered. Zib, who had never considered the voice of the earth, screamed. Mud flowed into her mouth. She screamed harder. Avery clung to her, his own mouth stubbornly shut, his face jammed against her shoulder, like denial could somehow change the situation unfolding around them. There had been no time to see how far the fall would be, no way to brace for it or to cushion the landing to come. There was only dropping through the air, surrounded by a sticky rainbow of taffy slime, out of control.

For the first time, Zib realized that "adventure" was

not always another way of saying "an exciting new experience" but could also be a way of saying "bad things happening very quickly, with no way to make them stop." She held tight to Avery, who had already known that sometimes adventures could be cruel, who had already known enough to be afraid.

Neither of them could see the cliff they fell past, but if they had, they would have understood the mud a little better, for the stone was banded in pink and blue and purple, stripes of one color sitting atop the next, like something from a storybook. But storybooks didn't usually try to kill the people who read them, and as Avery and Zib plummeted through the air, they were both quite sure that they were going to die.

At the bottom of the cliff, the mud had formed a sticky, stripy pool, like the runoff from a candy machine. Avery and Zib tumbled down in a cascade of falling mud; they struck the surface together and sank like small, terrified stones into the terrible depths. Without Avery to press the mud from the grass above, the river stopped flowing, and the last of the mud fell after them with a sucking, slurping sound.

Everything was still. Everything was cold, and possible, and *finished*. Yes. There was a finality to the scene, as if the world had grown weary of two children on an unintentional adventure and simply declared their journeys to be over and finished, and not of any importance to anyone else in the world. Their parents would weep and wonder. Their classmates would stare at empty chairs and make up stories about what had happened to them, where they could possibly have gone. The police would search, and find nothing, for there would be nothing to find.

Too many adventures end with this sort of finality, which is terrible and true and all too probable. But Avery and Zib had been following the improbable road, had stepped upon it the instant they stepped away from the comforting fiction of a straight line and glittering bricks winding through the landscape. So it was that they had barely vanished beneath the surface of the mud when an entire murder of crows swooped down from the cliff-side above them, landing on the bank and falling into the shape of a girl.

Crows do not, as a rule, become little girls casually, and perhaps that was why this girl, who was midway between Avery and Zib in size, was still so clearly a crow. She had simply found a means of being a little girl at the same time. She wore a short dress of black feathers, glossy and sleek and growing out of her skin, so that removing them would have meant plucking her bloody. Her nose was sharper than a nose should have been, but her eyes were sharper still, so that it seemed she could see everything, no matter how well concealed, and have an opinion about it. Her lips were thin and her toes were long, gripping the ground like a crow's talons grip a scarecrow's shoulder.

"Hello?" she said, to the pool of striped mud. "Are you mud-breathers? Are you breathing the mud *right now*?"

The mud did not respond.

"I don't think you are, no, no, I don't think you are, you looked like human children, lots of things can look like human children, but only the gnomes can look like human children *and* breathe mud, and you didn't look like gnomes. Gnomes would have been laughing more. Happy things, gnomes are, when they get to ride a mudslide someplace new. I don't think you can breathe down there."

The mud did not respond.

The girl who was a crow who was a girl frowned with her thin lips, leaning forward until the tip of her nose almost touched the surface of the mud. "Are you drowning? Don't say anything if you're drowning, and I'll know that means 'yes.'" She paused, a quizzical look flashing across her face. "But you probably don't *want* to be drowning, do you? You didn't look like you wanted to be drowning when you fell. Do you want to be saved? I want to save you, but if I do, you'll have to face the consequences, and maybe you don't want that."

The mud did not respond.

The crow girl straightened up, so that she was standing as straight as she could. Her arms drew up against her sides as she did, folding naturally into the shape of wings, for all that they didn't have any feathers on them, for all that she still had fingers, and hands, and other things an ordinary crow wouldn't have at all.

"I think I should save you," she said. "If you're angry, remember, you're the ones who didn't tell me not to, and if you don't like the consequences, well, they're probably better than being lost at the bottom of a mudslide, belly full of silt and lungs full of sorrow. Probably, probably, probably."

She bobbed her head, once, twice, three times, and then she dove into the pool of mud, vanishing quite completely. There was a long moment of silence before a bubble broke the surface, popping with a wet splattering sound, sending mud flying in all directions. The silence returned.

Then, with a gasp and a groan and a yell of triumph, the crow girl's head broke the surface. She had one arm wrapped around Avery, and one arm wrapped around Zib, and both of them started coughing and spitting out mud as soon as they were in the open air.

"Hold on, hold on," chattered the crow girl. "We're closer to there than we are to anywhere else, but you have to hold on."

Inch by inch, she pulled them to the shore. She flung Avery onto the bank first. He rolled away from the pool, coughing up more mud, so that it ran down his chin in cascades of pink and blue and purple. His shirt, which had been so white and so pristine and so perfect, was covered in swirls of color, so that he looked like he was wearing the results of a half-finished taffy pull. He lay there, limp and dripping, and watched with dull eyes as the crow girl maneuvered Zib to the pool's edge.

Zib's hair, that remarkable, untamable mass of curls and frizzes, was plastered down by the mud, forming a hard shell, like a helmet, like a jawbreaker. She barely looked like Zib without it to stand sentry for the rest of her. It was strange, strange, strange to look at her and not see her hair first. Avery closed his eyes. He didn't want to look at strange things anymore. He wanted to look at simple, ordinary things, things he already knew how to understand.

"This won't do," chided a new voice. "No, this won't do at *all*. Stay here, all right? Stay here, and I'll make it better."

There was a wet splatting sound, like a bag of laundry being thrown onto concrete. It was followed by the sound of wings, so many wings, uncountable wings clawing at the sky.

"Avery?"

The voice was Zib's, but it was barely a whisper. It was so close. Avery reached out, eyes still closed, and stopped when he felt his fingertips brush something solid.

"Avery, I'm scared."

"I'm scared too," he whispered, and somehow, that made it better. If they were both scared together, maybe things weren't so scary after all. Fear was a large and terrible monster, but fear could be conquered if enough people stood up against it.

They lay there in silence. For how long, neither of them could say, but they felt the mud hardening all over their bodies, until they couldn't have moved if they had wanted to. That should have been worrisome: Avery didn't like being dirty, and Zib didn't like being still, and here they were being both dirty *and* still, and they had no way to stop it. But they were so tired, and the sun was so warm, and maybe it was better to wait for the stranger who had rescued them to come back. Maybe it was safer.

The sound of wings drifted over them, distant at first, but growing louder and louder, until it felt like they were at the center of a thunderstorm made entirely of birds. Then, without warning, water came pouring from the sky above them, soaking them both to the skin in an instant. Zib sat up with a gasp, shaking water out of her hair, which immediately stood at attention, like she had turned into a lightning rod under her sphere of mud and silence. Avery sat up more slowly, and watched in awe as the unwanted colors bled out of his shirt and ran down to the muddy ground, which was quickly washing clear, revealing itself as a great stone symbol.

It was made of brick, red brick and black brick and those strange glittering bricks that had comprised the road that wasn't the improbable road, not really. Avery squinted at it, trying to understand. It was a sword, he thought, a sword with vast black wings fanning out from where the hilt should have been, and looking at it made him feel cold in a way he couldn't understand, because the rain was warm, and he was free, and he shouldn't have been cold.

Zib, meanwhile, sprang to her feet and gaped up at the sky, where crows—so many crows, a flock of crows, a murder of crows—circled around a dwindling, captive cloud. It was bruise-dark with rain, and lightning rippled across its surface as the crows darted in, nimbly avoiding the sparks of light and power, pecking its surface to send more water cascading down until the last of the mud was gone and the last of the cloud burst with a soft, sad popping sound.

The crows continued to circle, but as they circled they spiraled lower and lower, finally coming together, wings and bodies blending, black feathers flying, and somehow compressing themselves into the shape of a girl just their age.

The girl landed in a crouch, looking more like a wild thing than a child. Slowly she straightened, until she was standing a little taller than Avery, a little shorter than Zib, slotting into the space they made between them like it had been measured out to her specifications.

She had black hair and yellow eyes, and a dress made of black feathers that ended just above her knees. Her feet were bare and her nails were long and raggedy, like no one had ever trimmed them but let them grow until they could be used to climb the walls of the world. Avery looked at her and felt fear run all through him, cold and biting. Zib looked at her and thought she was the most wonderful thing in the entire world.

"Who *are* you?" asked Zib, all awe.

Avery had to swallow the urge to pull her away. She would stay there forever if he let her, of that much he was sure: she was so enchanted by this stranger, by this *adventure,* that she would never realize when she was in danger, and without her, he would never be able to go home. He was already forgetting that she had saved him, or done her best to save him, when the mud began to flow. Fear has a way of doing that to people.

"I'm a Crow Girl," said the stranger. She cocked her head. "Who are you?"

"I'm Avery, and this is Zib," said Avery. "Please, do you know where we are?"

"Why, this is the Up-and-Under, of course, and the Kingdom of the Queen of Swords," said the Crow Girl. She cocked her head in the opposite direction. "You must not be very clever, if you don't even know where you are. I blame the shoes."

"Shoes?" asked Zib, glancing down at her own stocking-clad toes. She didn't like this stranger, this Crow Girl, saying that she wasn't clever. She'd been plenty clever since climbing over the wall. Not knowing where she was wasn't a failure of cleverness, it was a failure of the people who were supposed to make the maps.

"Shoes." The Crow Girl held up her bare left foot and waggled her toes extravagantly. "If you can't feel where you're going, how will you ever know where you've been? Skies for wings and roads for feet, that's what the world is made of."

"How can something be up *and* under?" asked Avery. He had many more questions clawing at his throat, like "How were you just a flock of crows?" and "Why does your dress look like feathers?" and "Why am I so afraid of the symbol on the ground?" All of them felt too big and too wild and too *strange,* like asking them would change the world in a way it couldn't come back from. Better to ask the obvious, and maybe start to understand a little better what was going on.

"Up a tree's still under the sky," said the Crow Girl. "Here in the Up-and-Under, we're both things at once, always, and we're never anything in-between. It's good here. We're happy." A thin edge of strain came into her voice. She sounded like a little kid trying to claim that they hadn't stolen the last of the cookies. "We're all happy, always, because that's what it means to be in the Up-and-Under. Now that you're here, you'll be happy too."

"How do you know we're not from here?" asked Zib.

"If you were from here, you'd know where you were," said the Crow Girl. "You'd understand. You wouldn't be asking questions and questions and questions, like a bunch of chicks just out of the nest. It's fine not knowing things. Not knowing things means you have room to learn, and learning's about the most important thing there is, so the more ignorant you are, the more important you can be. But first step is saying that you know you don't know. Pretending to know things you don't never helped anyone."

"We were looking for the Impossible City," said Avery. "A man we met near the Forest of Borders said that the Queen of Wands would be able to give us an ending and send us home if we went there. Do you know which way the Impossible City is from here?"

"People certainly do like the word 'of' around here," said Zib. "Of this and of that."

"I like 'if' better," said the Crow Girl. She fixed Avery

with one yellow eye. "Are you sure you want an ending? Endings are tricky things. They wiggle and writhe like worms, and once you have them, you can't give them back again. You can hang them on hooks and sail the seas for sequels, if you realize you don't like where your story stopped, but you'll always have had an ending, and there will always be people who won't follow you past that line. You lose things when you have an ending. Big things. Important things. Better not to end at all, if you can help it."

"I didn't ask to begin," protested Avery. "All I wanted to do was go to school and take my spelling test and spell all the words right. I don't like mud and I don't like falling and I don't like clouds steered by crows and I don't like birds turning into girls!" He clapped his hands over his mouth, eyes going wide as he realized that he had said more than he intended to.

The Crow Girl turned her head back and forth, looking at him first out of one eye, and then out of the other. "Do you like drowning?" she asked. "Because you were awfully close to drowning. You fell out of the lands of the King of Coins and into the lands of the Queen of Swords. Earth and air together make for unquiet bedfellows. If I hadn't decided to be a girl instead of a murder of crows, you would have gone down, down, down, and you wouldn't even have joined the Drowned Boys, not here, not so very far from the sea."

"I'm sorry," said Avery. "I didn't mean . . ." And he stopped, because he didn't know what else to say.

Zib stepped forward, holding out her open hand. In

it was her lucky seashell. All the mud had been rinsed away, leaving it gleaming. "Here," she said. "A present. To thank you for helping us. Do you like presents?"

"Everyone likes presents," said the Crow Girl. She inched closer. "For me? Really? No tricks or treachery?"

"No," said Zib. "Just a present."

"A present!" The Crow Girl snatched the seashell out of Zib's hand, turning it greedily over in her hands before tucking it away in the feathers of her dress, where it vanished without a trace. She looked at Zib. "I'll give you a present, too. I'll walk with you, because the ending you'll find *with* me is better than the ending you'll find *without* me. Won't that be nice?"

"Yes," said Zib.

Avery, who didn't know the answer, said nothing at all.

FIVE

THE BUMBLE BEAR
AND THE TANGLE

The rolling green hills and the bright glassine ribbon of the improbable road were high above them, on the other side of the mudslide, which had tapered off to nothing more than the occasional colorful plop. Avery and Zib stood side by side and looked glumly up at the cliff.

"I don't think I can climb that," said Zib. "My shoes are up there."

"I *know* I can't climb that," said Avery. "Quartz is up there. Do you think he'll come looking for us? Do you think he'll bring a rope?"

"Quartz?" asked the Crow Girl.

"A man who is also a boulder who told us we had to go to the Impossible City," said Zib.

"Oh," said the Crow Girl. "You met a royal gnome. He can't follow you here. Royal gnomes belong to the King of Coins, and the Queen doesn't like them much."

"But he was going with us to the Impossible City," protested Avery. "He wanted to see the Queen of Wands."

"Of course he did. The Queen of Wands favors fire, you see, and gnomes aren't born from fire, but they like the way it tingles. They're not afraid of her. Many of them love her very much, and some of them belong to her court. As long as she holds the City, the road is open to gnomes and salamanders, and not so much to sylphs and undines. The Queen of Swords and the King of Cups have to find ways around her barriers when they want to get anything done." The Crow Girl sobered. "Be careful of them."

"Of who?" asked Zib.

"The ways around," said the Crow Girl. "None of them are what they were, and it's hard to remember how to play fair when you don't remember where you left your heart."

"I don't understand any of this," said Avery. His stomach grumbled. He sighed. "I don't understand any of this *and* I'm hungry."

"I have an apple," said Zib.

"I know where we can find more than a napple," said the Crow Girl. "What's a napple? Is it some kind of cake? I would like to try the cake from wherever it is you came from."

"It's a kind of fruit," said Zib.

"Oh," said the Crow Girl. "Well, then, I shouldn't like to eat that at all, and you shouldn't want to eat it either. Come on, come on, both of you, come on." She jumped back, turned, and ran to the edge of the stone circle, where she paused and looked over her shoulder. "Are you coming?"

Avery and Zib hesitated.

"This seems very unsafe," said Avery.

"Yes," said Zib. "But that's what makes it improbable. Come on!" She scampered after the Crow Girl. After a moment, Avery followed her. There was nothing else for him to do.

At the edge of the stone circle was another cliff, this one high and sheer and terrifying. Set into the side of the cliff was a stone stairway, winding down toward the ground far, far below. The Crow Girl all but danced onto the steps, and kept dancing downward, toward the layer of mist that hung above the distant countryside. Zib followed more cautiously, and Avery followed more cautiously still, until they were like beads on a string, separated by great streaks of open distance.

The Crow Girl looked back several times, calling encouragement, but the wind took her words and whisked them away like prizes, keeping them from ever reaching the children. Zib watched the mist as it got closer, and the countryside as it began to form houses and farms and great flower gardens, hedge mazes and fields and other lovely, enticing things. Avery watched the back of Zib's head. Her hair, wild and tangled and ridiculous as it was, had somehow become an anchor. It didn't change.

It was always improbable, always doing as it liked, with no regard for anyone around it. If he focused on her hair, he could pretend they were still on the road, where there had been no reason to fall, where—if he somehow *had* fallen—he wouldn't have tumbled to his doom.

The mist, when they passed through it, was cold and cloying and smelled like lavender, like the sachets Avery's mother liked to put in with the fresh linens. Breathing it made him feel faintly homesick. He wanted his mother to tuck him into bed and tell him he'd been a good boy. He wanted his father to clap him on the shoulder and call him "sport" and "champ" and "scout." He wanted to be anywhere but here.

But Zib . . . ah, Zib. She would have told anyone who asked that she was happy at home, and she wouldn't have been lying, because she had always been happy at home, in the same way a bird who has grown up in a cage can be quietly, unwittingly happy there. She had based happiness on the way she felt when she looked at the sensible, probable walls and went through the sensible, probable patterns of her days. Now, though, now she felt like she might finally be learning to understand what happy really was. Happy was descending a cliff with a new friend in front of her and a new friend behind her, and so many wonderful things to see, and do, and discover. Happiness was the Up-and-Under.

Bit by bit, the distance fell behind them, until they could see the bottom of the stairs. It ended at a wide tunnel made of briars and brambles. The Crow Girl made a sound of wordless delight and dashed forward, skipping down the last of the stairs and diving for the tunnel. She was almost inside when a vast paw darted out of the darkness, claws as long as dinner knives swiping for the Crow Girl's chest.

This time, her wordless exclamation was less delight and more dismay. She danced backward. The paw swiped again, and the Crow Girl broke into a hundred black-winged pieces, exploding into the murder of crows she had originally been. They scattered into the briars and branches, cawing angrily.

Zib froze, and stayed frozen as Avery slammed into her, sending them both teetering. They stayed there, staring, as the great beast came stalking out of the shadows, and roared.

The sound was as wide as the sky and as deep as the sea. It echoed; it challenged; it set the hairs on the back of Avery's neck standing on edge. The hairs on the back of Zib's neck were already standing on edge, as was all the rest of the hair on her head, but her skin made up the difference, pulling itself into painful lumps of gooseflesh. The beast roared again, and it was like the world was shaking, no longer content to be a stationary thing.

As for the beast itself, it was a thing that befit its roar, which is to say, huge and terrible and strange. If Avery had been asked to guess at what it was, on penalty of being thrown to the creature, he would have called it some sort of bear, for it was hulking and shaggy and possessed of terrible claws and even more terrible jaws, which bristled with truly terrible teeth. Had Zib been asked the same question, she would have called it some sort of nightmare bee, for it was striped yellow and black, and its backside tapered into a wicked point, a stinger the size of a fisherman's harpoon. They would both have been right, in their own ways, and they would both have been wrong.

The beast roared a third time. Then it coughed into one paw, fixed the children with a cold, calculating eye, and said, "You are trespassing on my path. What will you give me not to kill you?"

Avery did not consider himself a terribly brave person. Still, he knew a wrong thing when he heard it. "This isn't your path," he said, stepping forward, so that he and Zib were clustered together on the same stone step. "At the top, we saw the sigil of the Queen of Swords. She wouldn't give the road that leads to her sign to someone else. I think you're pretending to own something that doesn't belong to you. I think the Queen of Swords would be very interested in hearing about that."

The crows cackled with laughter as the beast took a thudding step backward, safely away from the children.

"Maybe that's so and maybe that's not so," it grumbled. "Maybe this is her path, but I'm still a beast of the brambles, and I'm allowed to eat. So what will you give me not to kill you?"

"Nothing," said Avery. "You're too big to climb these steps, and we can just go back the way we came, away from you. You won't be able to hurt us."

"No, but you won't be able to reach whatever it is you were trying to reach," said the beast. "What will you give me to let you pass?"

"I don't see why we should have to give you anything," said Avery. "The road isn't yours."

"Perhaps not, but these are mine." The beast held up one vast paw, flexing it so that its claws slid out, sharp and gleaming. "And these are mine." The beast bared its teeth, showing them in all their terrible glory. "The Queen is often cold and often cruel, and she appreciates those qualities in her monsters. She will not blame me for following my nature."

The crows in the brambles shrieked and cawed but showed no sign of transforming back into the Crow Girl, or of somehow harrying the monster away. Bravery has its limits, no matter what the world.

Zib tugged on her hair, which sprang right back into place when she let it go. "I don't think you're a monster," she said. "You're talking. You're threatening, but you're still talking, not just attacking. I don't think you're a monster at all."

"Some monsters speak, child," said the beast. "The very best monsters speak like kings and queens, eloquent and alluring, and the trick is learning not to listen. If you listen to *those* monsters, they'll have your heart out before you realize how much danger you're in."

"Do you have a name?"

"They call me the Bumble Bear, because I am big as a bear, and hatched in a hive among all the other bees. It was golden honey and golden afternoons, when

I was young; it was all sweetness and nectar. But the Queen of Swords had need of a monster, and so she plucked me from the honeycomb and breathed vastness onto me, took my wings and traded them for teeth and claws and hunger. I am what I am because she wanted me so, and I love her for seeing the potential in me, and I despise her for taking me away from my family. She'll change you if she catches you, little human children. She'll make you over into her dearest desires, and not understand why you might want anything else, even for a moment. Queens are cruel monsters. They eat and eat and are never full, and they leave lesser beasts in their wake. So I ask again, for my stomach aches and my temper shortens: what will you give me to let you pass?"

"We don't have anything," said Avery. "We're *children*." Because Avery, of course, had been allowed the luxury of thinking that childhood was somehow sacred: that it somehow compelled the world to be kind. There had always been people who criticized his parents for the way they raised him, who said that he was an adult in miniature, with his starched shirts and his sensible shoes, but he had never once worried about where dinner was going to come from, or what would happen if he trusted an adult's word.

Zib, however . . . her parents had done their best, and they had never been bad parents, not intentionally, not exactly. But they had been little more than children themselves when she was born, and her father was always tired from driving buses and being a parent to other people's children, while her mother made her living with dreams, and sometimes forgot that children needed things like lunches and snacks and shoes without holes in the bottoms. They did their best. Their house was filled with love. That didn't mean Zib had ever, for an hour, for an instant, had the casual faith in the difference between childhood and adulthood that Avery clung to so fiercely.

"What do you want?" she asked, cautiously.

"Something good," said the Bumble Bear. "Something you'll remember. Something you'll regret. I could take the freckles from your cheeks, or the frizzes from your hair. They would look very fine in my fur."

Zib clutched the sides of her head, horrified. Her freckles were her own, and she didn't want them to be gone, but more, her hair was the one part of her that had never listened to anyone else, not ever, not since she was born. She had been told to be good, be quiet, sit still, behave, and she had done her best to listen, over and over again, even when the people speaking didn't have her best interests at heart. Like most of us, Zib had only ever wanted to be loved, and had always been willing to compromise to make it more possible. Her hair, however—her hair knew no compromise, gave no quarter. It was wild and dizzy and ecstatic, like lightning striking the same patch of sand over and over again for nothing more than the joy of kissing the world. Without it, she would be someone else. Maybe someone who people would like better, listen to more; maybe someone who had more friends, whose parents were better about making breakfasts and buying clean socks. If her hair finally calmed down, maybe she could be Hepzibah after all.

She didn't *want* to be Hepzibah. She wanted to be Zib, Zib, Zib, for as long as she could, and she certainly didn't want to give Zib to a beast of the brambles, however cruelly that beast had been treated by a queen.

"Not those," she said.

"What, then? The contents of your pockets? The shine from your eyes? You have to give me something, or I'll never let you pass, and wherever it is you thought you were going will have to wait forever to have you." The Bumble Bear considered its own claws. "The choice is yours. I can stand here as long as anything."

Shine . . . "The shine from Avery's shoes," Zib blurted, not seeing the horrified, betrayed look Avery gave her. "Could you take that?"

"I can take *anything*," said the Bumble Bear. It looked at Avery for a moment. Then it nodded, apparently satisfied. "Yes. That will do. Come here, children, and do not be afraid. We're bound by a bargain now, you and I, and that makes us the next best thing to brothers, at least until that bargain is fulfilled. I could no more do you harm than I could pluck the eyes from my own head and still see the sky."

"I don't want—" began Avery, and stopped as the Bumble Bear looked at him.

"Do you wish to challenge the bargain?" it asked. "You can say the girl has no right to deal for you, of course you can say that, and then I will have to treat her as a thief." It smiled, showing all of its teeth, as the crows in the brambles cawed fury and fear. "It would be my pleasure."

"N-no," said Avery. "She has the right to deal for us both."

Zib looked at him with gratitude and joy. Avery didn't look at her at all.

"Then come, children, and continue," said the Bumble Bear.

They descended the last of the stone steps side by shaking side, and when they reached the beast, with its teeth and its claws and its stinger, they stopped, waiting for the hammer to fall. The Bumble Bear bent, breathing on Avery's shoes. It breathed and breathed, exhaling like a gale, and when it finally stopped, it looked pleased with itself. It stepped back and to the side, leaving them room to pass.

Avery did not move. Zib grabbed him by the arm and dragged him with her past the Bumble Bear, into the sheltering darkness of the briars. They were well out of reach, and almost out of sight, when a voice spoke behind them.

"Wait."

Zib turned. Avery did not.

The Bumble Bear, while still a beast, was not a monster; it was only a tired animal, looking at them with eyes that had seen too many terrible things to ever close peacefully. "You walk in the Tangle now, and the Tangle belongs to the Queen of Swords. I have threatened you, yes. I would have eaten you, had you refused to pay me, and I would devour you now, swallow you down in an instant, if you came too close. But I am an honest beast. I eat because my belly is empty, and I guard because I have no hive, no cave, only this narrow territory to call my own. The Queen of Swords will not devour you, but she will eat you all the same. Be careful, children. If you can't be careful, come back to me, and I will swallow you, and we will be together always, and you will remember who you are."

"Thank you," said Zib gravely. Avery said nothing at all. The two children walked on, and the murder of crows poured after them, deeper into the twisted briars, until the Bumble Bear, great beast of bargains and barriers, was left alone once more.

SIX

THE ROAD RETURNS

The path through the Tangle was hard-packed earth, almost clay. It smelled of mud and rain and all the other good things Zib remembered from the creek, and it was soft under her stockinged feet, making it easier to keep walking even though her shoes were long since lost. She glanced nervously around, all too aware that she was surrounded by the sort of sharp thorns that were entirely unpleasant to step on, and kept walking.

Avery plodded, not speaking, not looking to the left or right. Zib stole looks in his direction, feeling dimly as if he, too, had become a sort of sharp thorn, something she could easily prick herself upon.

When the first of the glowing bricks appeared in the

dirt, Zib gasped and exclaimed, "The improbable road! Why, Avery, it's found us even here! I didn't know roads could do that!"

The crows, which had been flying merrily all around them, began to flock together, becoming a twister of black wings and black feathers and wind, until they finally solidified into the body of the Crow Girl, who laughed and danced backward, causing more bricks to light up in the muddy ground.

"The road can follow you anywhere, as long as you're following the rules," she said. "It can find a feather in a hurricane or a bubble at the bottom of the sea. Two children and a Crow Girl, that's no trouble at all!"

"Why," said Avery, in a dull, soft voice. The word was not a question on his lips: it was a condemnation, a quiet statement of fact.

The Crow Girl cocked her head to the side. "Why what? Why is the road like this? The road goes everywhere in the Up-and-Under, into the clouds and down to the depths, because the road is for everyone, and something for everyone needs to be everywhere, or it isn't really for everyone at all. A garden behind a gate isn't everybody's garden, no matter what the gardeners may try to say. No, it isn't for everyone at all."

"Why didn't you help us?" Avery lifted his head and looked at her, as bleak as a midwinter morning. The sparkle, tame and tranquil as it was, had gone out of his eyes; he was a shadow of himself. "You were there, you were *right there*, and you could have helped us with the

Bumble Bear, but you didn't help us at all. You stayed crows in the brambles, and you let it threaten us, and scare us, and t-take things from us. You're no friend at all. You're a *coward*."

"Everything with wings is a coward," said the Crow Girl. "Even the things that want to be brave, the hawks and eagles and vultures and pelicans, they're all cowards. To have wings is to know how to fly away." She paused before adding, thoughtfully, "Maybe emus aren't cowards. They have wings, but they've forgotten how to fly. Maybe they can learn to be brave."

"Is that why you didn't help us?" asked Avery. "Because you were afraid?" Angry as he was, hurt as he was, he could understand some of what it meant to be afraid. Avery was a clean, polite, patient child in a world where children were encouraged to be those things at home, but something entirely other in the company of their peers. He had never mastered pretending to be something or someone that he wasn't.

"Oh, no," said the Crow Girl. "Even a coward can harry and strike. Sometimes it's better to be a coward. The brave rush in, the brave think they know what's what and who's who, and the brave get buried in soft green moss, with stones to rest their heads upon. I'm not a creature of stone or moss, though, and a coward can be careful. Cowards take their time. Cowards find the way that's right, instead of the way that's easy."

"Then why . . ."

"The Queen of Swords made me," said the Crow

Girl. Her voice was soft, and simple, and sad. She looked at the children in front of her, wrapping her bare arms around her feathered body as if she thought she could hold herself in place. "She didn't steal me from a hive or anything like that. I went willing, we all go willing, because she offered me transformation, transfiguration, transmutation from something I didn't want to be into something I did. I was someone else before I came to her, and I wasn't happy then, but I'm happy now, yes, I'm happy now. I serve the Queen and I'm happy. She loves me so, she'll keep me forever."

"The Bumble Bear belonged to her," said Zib slowly.

"So many things do," said the Crow Girl. "I didn't know it would be there, I promise that. There was never a beast of any kind at that bramble break before. The Queen must have heard us coming and placed a guard."

"Why would she do that if she loves you?" asked Zib.

"Because she wants to love you, too. She wants to love all the children who walk the improbable road, to gather them close and keep them warm and safe and free from the temptations of the Impossible City, the allure of the alchemical aurora. She wants us to be wild and bestial and home forever, nevermore to roam." The Crow Girl glanced around, suddenly anxious, suddenly seeming more like a wild creature than she ever had before, like the part of her that was human was less important than the part of her that was bird. She stepped closer to Avery and Zib, bobbing her head low, so that her words would be spilled only between the three of them and not into the wider world.

Avery and Zib found themselves leaning in to catch every syllable, not allowing any of them to fall to the muddy earth, to the returning road. These were crumbs for their ears, and theirs alone.

"I can't fight what belongs to the Queen, for they are my brothers and my sisters and my siblings all, and she doesn't allow fighting in her family; she judges it most harshly, and when she punishes us, it aches for years on end. So no, I couldn't help you against her beast, and I won't help you against any other beasts we happen to encounter, not when they belong to her. She would love you too, if you allowed her to, and her love would be everything you had ever wanted, and nothing that you needed. If you trust her, you'll never make it home. You'll never have your ending, good or bad or in-between, for all endings here belong to the Queen of Swords, and she doesn't share. Be careful. Be cowards. Courage belongs to the brave and the foolish, and they are always, always the first to fall before her glory."

The Crow Girl straightened abruptly, dancing back onto the glimmering bricks of the improbable road, a bright smile on her thin, hard-lipped mouth. "I promised you food! Better than a napple! Come, children, come, cowards, come, come, come!"

Zib, hesitant but hungry, began to follow, and stopped as Avery reached out and grabbed her wrist. She looked at his hand, tight and trembling, holding her fast; then she looked at his face, and nearly shied away from the wildness there.

"We should run," he said. "While she's distracted."

"Where?" she asked. "There's only one tunnel through the briars, and the Bumble Bear is at one end of it, and the other end is ahead of us, with the Crow Girl in our way. Even if we went back—even if we *could* go back—there's nothing but stairs and a mountain to fall from, and a stone circle to shiver and starve in. The Queen of Swords doesn't know we're here. She doesn't want us yet, she can't. I need food, and a good place to sit, and something to cover my feet. Let me go, Avery, and walk. We have to walk if we're to reach the Impossible City."

Reluctantly, Avery released her wrist. "This is the wrong thing to do," he said.

"Maybe it is and maybe it isn't," said Zib. "It's what we have right now."

She turned back to the road, the scattered, glimmering bricks all the brighter now that the Crow Girl had stepped on them and reminded them that they had a job to do. She began to follow it, making the bricks grow brighter still. Avery watched, trembling. He wanted to be brave. He wanted to stand alone in the brambles, to let the darkness come down around him, and to know that he was not afraid.

He was afraid. He was so very afraid. Something rustled in the brambles and he was running, racing after Zib and the Crow Girl, running through the Tangle until the tunnel of briars ended around him and he was standing in sunlight once again. He stopped, chest heaving, heart pounding, and looked around himself with wide, bewildered eyes.

The improbable road was no longer made of scattered bricks. It was shining and complete, stretching ahead of him in a pearlescent ribbon that wove between berry bushes and high trees whose branches were alive with birds he had never seen before and couldn't name. The ground to either side of the road was windswept and dusted with sparse, sere-looking grass, like the fields at the end of the growing season. Zib was up ahead, plucking bright pink berries from a bush twice as tall as she was. The Crow Girl was nowhere to be seen.

Avery stopped in the middle of the road, scowling. Zib looked content, almost, like this was normal, ordinary—like this was the way the world was supposed to be, and not proof that something had gone terribly, horribly, awfully wrong. Roads weren't supposed to glow, or to follow people. Flocks of crows weren't supposed to turn into girls, and girls weren't supposed to turn into flocks of crows. Berries weren't supposed to be as pink as sugar candy, and somehow that was the worst offense of all, because it was such a *small* one. Everything else had been a huge offense, mudslides and monsters and boulders that talked and owls that gave advice. It had been like walking in a terrible, complicated, frustrating dream. But this . . .

Berries were simple. Berries were small, ordinary

things, served in bowls with cream for dessert, or maybe baked into pies. They didn't belong in dreams, and yet there they were, staining Zib's fingers and lips with their juices. If there were berries here, this wasn't a dream, and if this wasn't a dream, it was really happening. Avery didn't want it to be really happening. He didn't want that at all.

"Avery!"

He blinked, and focused. Zib had seen him. She was waving one pink-stained hand, a bright smile on her face.

"They're safe to eat," she said, and held out her other hand, showing him the berries cupped in her palm. "They're called bonberries, and they grow everywhere around here."

"Where's the Crow Girl?" he asked. His stomach rumbled and grumbled, reminding him that it had been a long time and a lot of walking since breakfast. He tried to push the feeling aside. He didn't want to eat those berries. He didn't want to *look* at them. They made the Up-and-Under too real, and they didn't belong here.

"She went to get us some fish and bigger fruit," said Zib. "She told me to stay here for when you came out of the brambles, because you'd want to know where she was."

Avery scowled again. "I don't want to eat anything she brings. I don't want to put this place in my stomach and let it be a part of me. I want to *leave*. I want to go *home*. Why are you so happy? You shouldn't be happy. This is a bad place."

"This is an adventure," said Zib. "Shouldn't you be happy? I thought everyone wanted an adventure."

"Not me!" Avery realized he was shouting. He realized he didn't know how to stop. Most of all, he realized that he didn't want to. "I want to go to school and go home and do my chores and go to bed and be *safe*! I want to tell my father about my day and have him laugh and say I'm smart and good and just the sort of son he always hoped he'd have! I want my books and my room and my things and *not this*!" He stomped his foot for emphasis, then ground out, every word a stone: "I. Want. My. Shoes. To. *Shine*."

Zib's face fell. "Oh. I—"

"Don't. I don't want to talk to you. I want to go home." Avery began to pace from one side of the road to the other, turning back every time it seemed like he might touch the windswept ground.

The berries that had been so sweet a few seconds before didn't taste very good anymore. Zib looked at the squashed pink mass in her hand, wrinkled her nose, and flung it as far from the road as she could. Then she sat and hugged her knees to her chest, watching Avery pace back and forth across the rainbow sheen of the improbable road, his hands in his pockets and a frown on his face.

Avery paced. Zib began counting silently to one hundred, ticking off his steps. When she reached a hundred, she started again, and again, until it seemed like she had always been counting, until it seemed like surely, she'd counted enough.

"Are you done being angry with me yet?" she called.

"No," he replied, voice sullen. "You shouldn't have done that."

Zib didn't have to ask what she'd done: it was obvious. "We needed to give something to the Bumble Bear if we wanted it to let us pass. It couldn't be my slingshot, and it couldn't be your ruler. The shine from your shoes was something we could lose. It didn't hurt us."

"It hurt *me*," said Avery. He finally stopped pacing and turned to look at her again, expression bleak. Something about him seemed so lost that Zib stopped *looking* at him and started *seeing* him, which was something else altogether. People *look* at things all day long and never really see them; look at the shelves without seeing their contents, look at the houses without seeing the people who live inside.

Look at their friends and neighbors without seeing the harmony and horror in their hearts.

Without their shine, Avery's shoes were ordinary brown leather, like any kid out on the playground might be wearing. They didn't reflect him anymore. They were too scuffed to reflect anything. His shirt seemed just a little less starched without them reflecting its crispness; his hair seemed just a little less combed. He looked like an ordinary boy. Zib hadn't known him for very long, but she already knew that that was wrong.

She felt fear tickle her ribs. If they had to lose themselves to walk this road, would it ever really be able to lead them home?

"I have birthday money," she said. "I keep it in a pickle jar I bury in the backyard. I move it every weekend, in case pirates come looking for the buried treasure. I'll dig it up when we get home, and we'll buy you a new pair of shoes. The brightest, shiniest shoes you ever saw. Shoes like stars."

"Stars fall down a lot," said Avery.

"So every time you fall down, you can make a wish on your shoes, and it'll come true," said Zib.

She sounded so earnest that it startled a laugh out of him, and that laugh broke the shell of his anger, letting it all leak out and away. He laughed again, happier now. Maybe it didn't matter if these shoes were shiny: there were other shoes in the world. Shinier shoes, even, shoes like stars.

"Buy me shoes and we're square," said Avery.

"Deal," said Zib. "Do you want some berries now?"

Avery's stomach growled, and he found that indeed, he did.

When the Crow Girl returned, on foot—becoming a murder of crows was a useful thing in many situations, but not when she needed to carry a picnic hamper big enough to use both hands—she found the children with sticky pink mouths and sticky pink fingers, sitting contentedly in the shadow of a large berry bush. She cocked her head to the side, considering them.

This is not the Crow Girl's story: if ever that story were to be told, it would not begin in an ordinary town, or on an ordinary street. But she is important enough to this story that certain things must be said. First, that she meant well in all ways; second, that she was not well beloved of the Queen of Swords before she chose to rescue two children from a muddy grave; and third, that because she was both child and corvid, her heart was ever divided against itself, like a house with too many locked doors. She looked at Avery and Zib and felt a great longing wash over her. She wanted to be loved as carelessly as they were growing to love each other. She wanted to be comfortable enough to sit silently, berry juice on her fingers and the improbable road under her behind. Most of all, she wanted to spare them from the road ahead.

She was still standing there, trying to decide, when Avery saw her and waved a greeting. She blinked. Of the two of them, she had assumed that Zib would be happiest to see her, but Zib was watching a beetle crawl across a rock and hadn't noticed her at all. The Crow Girl smiled like the sun coming out and skipped toward the pair, holding up her picnic hamper.

"Fish!" she proclaimed. "Fish and bread and I promised you something better than a napple, didn't I? Well, here it is!" She set the hamper down with a thump and flipped its lid open, reaching in and pulling out what could have been a very small, pale, fleshy octopus, if it had possessed eyes, or suckers, or any of the other attributes that distinguish "octopus" from "a thing which has many tentacles."

Zib blinked. "What is it?"

"This is a flavor fruit!" said the Crow Girl triumphantly. She thrust it at Zib. "Here! Try!"

Zib looked dubiously at the flavor fruit, and had the distinct, unsettling impression that it was looking back at her. But the Crow Girl looked so proud, and somehow the thought of disappointing her was even more unsettling than the impression of being stared at by a bundle of tentacles. Cautiously, Zib reached out and took the fruit. It was soft and warm, with a surface that felt like the skin of a peach, lightly fuzzy in an almost animal way.

"How do I eat it?" asked Zib. "Is it like—" She stopped. The Crow Girl didn't know what an apple was. Why would she understand words like "banana" or "orange" or any of the other fruits Zib could ask about? This wasn't home. This wasn't anything like home. The longer they walked, the less like home the Up-and-Under seemed.

"You break off the arms, silly," said the Crow Girl. She grasped one of the flavor fruit's twisty tentacles and twisted, snapping it neatly off. The flesh of the fruit was white as bone or custard, pale and scentless. The Crow Girl sat back on her heels, beginning to gnaw the tentacle. She didn't remove the skin or check for seeds.

Cautiously, Zib grasped a tentacle and mimicked the Crow Girl's motion. It came off easily, as easily as plucking a ripe tomato from the plants in the backyard.

The Crow Girl nodded encouragement, and Zib raised the tentacle to her mouth. Then she gasped, eyes going wide.

"It tastes like my grandmother's gingerbread!" she said. "It's warm, and sweet, and— How is this possible?"

"Try another one," said the Crow Girl.

Zib greedily stuffed the rest of the tentacle into her mouth, reveling in the taste of every Christmas she had shared with her grandmother, molasses and spice and sugar. The flavor still clung to her teeth as she broke off another tentacle and took her first bite, only to gasp again.

"Ice cream at the beach in summer! *Strawberry* ice cream!"

"I don't know what a strawberry is, but I know ice cream," said the Crow Girl. She broke another tentacle off her flavor fruit, offering it to Avery. "Here. Try it and see!"

Avery frowned at the tentacle. He didn't like the look of it. But he liked being rude even less, and so he reached out took the tentacle, sticking the very tip of it into his mouth. Like Zib, his eyes went wide.

"It tastes like my mother's spaghetti," he said, wondering. "I can taste the garlic, and the tomato sauce, and the mushrooms. But . . . spaghetti doesn't taste like gingerbread or ice cream, not even a little. This can't be real."

"Flavor fruit was a gift from the Queen of Wands,

when she had to step aside from being summer and take her place in the Impossible City," said the Crow Girl. "She wanted to be sure that everyone would always be able to eat the things they like best in the world, because everybody needs a treat sometimes. You can't eat only flavor fruit—you still need fish and bread and other good things in your belly, or you'll get a stomachache—and that's why it's hard to grow. People would eat only it, if they had a choice."

"I guess that makes sense," said Avery, hungrily eyeing the fruit in the Crow Girl's hands. Zib was munching on hers, body slightly curved away, so that there was no chance she'd have to share.

The Crow Girl handed him the fruit. "All yours," she said magnanimously, before producing a third from the hamper. "We have to eat some fish and bread when we're done, though, or it'll be like eating all dessert and no dinner: hungry again an hour later, and ready for bed half an hour after that. How do children sleep, where you come from?"

"Um," said Avery. "We mostly just close our eyes and . . . do."

"Sometimes my parents let me take a sleeping bag into the backyard and I sleep where all the stars can see me," said Zib. "Once I woke up with a spider in my nose."

"That must have been very surprising for the spider," said the Crow Girl. "You stay all in one piece when you sleep? How queer. I don't know what I'd do if I had to be all one piece and try to rest at the same time. I think I'd shake myself apart even trying."

"We're always in one piece," said Avery.

"No one is *always* in one piece," said the Crow Girl. "Your heart wants one thing and your head wants something else and your lungs are pig-in-the-middle trying to argue with the both of them. Your spine wants to sit and your feet want to go and your hands want to grab, and they can't all have their way. No wonder you look so confused and cranky! When all the parts of me start arguing, I pull them apart until they calm down. You, though, you keep holding them together."

"We don't mind," said Zib. "I would think it very strange, if my hands and my feet went off in different directions at the same time."

"You get used to it," said the Crow Girl, and took a hearty bite of her own flavor fruit, smiling blissfully. "Carrion pie. Just like home."

Neither Zib nor Avery knew what that tasted like, and they didn't want to: they were happy to eat their own flavor fruit and then, once it was gone, to eat the fish and bread the Crow Girl had promised. The fish was juicy and sweet, roasted with unfamiliar greens and more of the little pink berries, which had burst as they cooked, spreading seeds across the fish's skin. They popped between the teeth, adding a delightful sensation to their supper. The bread was soft and fresh, and there was cheese and butter and oh! Such a lovely meal it was that both children quite forgot how much they wanted another flavor fruit, and simply ate what had been set in front of them.

When they were finished, the plates licked clean and the hamper empty and their bellies aching pleasantly, as they always did after a good meal, they sat back in comfortable quiet. Zib leaned until her head rested on Avery's shoulder, that insouciant hair brushing his cheek, and it seemed so right for her to be there that he didn't object.

"That was wonderful," he said, for his parents had always stressed the importance of remembering his manners. "Thank you. Did you cook it all yourself?"

"Oh, no," said the Crow Girl. "I stole it!"

Avery gasped. Zib sat bolt upright, and it seemed like her hair sat up even straighter, so that she looked like she'd been struck by lightning.

"*Stole* it?" asked Avery. "From *whom*?"

"Why, the Queen of Swords, of course. Everything here belongs to her. Every beast and briar, every hill and hearth. All the crows have to steal if we want to eat. The Queen doesn't mind. She's the one who made us this way, and she knows that we don't mean any harm by it." The Crow Girl cocked her head thoughtfully to the side. "Although I suppose if you still want to get to the Impossible City, we should start walking again. The Queen doesn't like things she doesn't own, so she'll come to try and own you soon. It's the only way to keep everything exactly as she wants it and not a bit as she doesn't."

"So you stole our lunch from the woman who doesn't

want us here, and you don't think that's bad," said Zib. She scrambled to her feet, one sock snagging on the uneven brick and pulling away from her foot, leaving her toes bare. "That's all you stole, though, right? You didn't take anything else?"

"Only one other thing. Catch!" The Crow Girl reached into her dress and pulled out a key, tossing it to Avery, who caught it without thinking. Then he gasped, nearly dropping it again.

It was a key, yes, but a key a foot long, carved from what looked like a single piece of bone. The surface was covered in scrimshaw swirls, showing two children walking the long length of a ribbon road. To make the point even clearer, the lines of the road had been picked out in mother-of-pearl, so that it glittered and gleamed against the white. It was stark and terrible and beautiful, all at the same time, for all things can be many things, under the right conditions.

"It's a skeleton key," said the Crow Girl smugly. "They're supposed to be guarded, oh yes, locked away from the likes of me and us and we all together, but I got one. I snatched it and cached it and now all we need to do is find the lock that fits it and you can move on to the protectorate of the Queen of Wands. She isn't there now, no, she isn't there at all, what with the Impossible City needing all her time, but if we can't find it—" Her face fell. She finished, almost in a whisper, "If we can't find it, we have to go the long way round, through the protectorate of the King of Cups. You don't want that, not at all. You want to stay safe and dry and well away from *him*."

"Why do you have so many kings and queens around here, and why do we have to be afraid of half of them?" demanded Zib.

"Well, because if you *belonged* to one of them, you wouldn't have to be afraid of them, and maybe you'd be afraid of the other half, which can be a nice change." The Crow Girl stood and stretched, yawning at the same time. "Up, up, up. We need to be moving before we decide that sleeping would be better. Nothing can force you off the improbable road, not even queens and kings, but that doesn't mean they can't try, and sometimes the road goes on adventures of its own, and then you're stuck. So get up, up, up. It's time to walk."

Zib was already standing. She turned to offer her hands to Avery, who took them and let himself be pulled from the ground. He was still holding the skeleton key. She shied away from it, dimly aware that she was glad *he* had been chosen as its guardian, and not her at all.

"If you could fly, this would be easier, but if you could fly, we wouldn't be here, so I suppose we'll work with what we have," said the Crow Girl. "On you go!"

Avery and Zib moved closer together, Zib's hand still holding tight to one of his. Without a word or a glance between them, they began walking.

The protectorate of the Queen of Swords was beautiful: of that there could be no question. Birds circled overhead, and other shapes that were almost birds but not quite. Avery squinted and thought they might be dragons, or winged people, soaring on currents he was too far down to feel. The Crow Girl's comments about flight seemed more reasonable than they had before he saw that, and he shivered.

All around them were rolling hills and trees with high, straight branches, perfect for climbing or for roosting in. As he thought that, two things happened at essentially the same time, so that no matter which we mention first, we are getting something out of order. So:

What he had first taken to be a particularly low cloud, snuggled tight against the trunk of one of the tall roosting trees, stirred itself, opened eyes as startlingly blue as a summer afternoon, and spread its wings, revealing itself to be a snowy owl the same impossible size as Meadowsweet. It launched itself into the air, gliding silently over the improbable road, circling the trio twice before setting down in front of them, and:

The improbable road, which had never been a straight line—had always been a curving, twisting thing, like a length of ribbon thrown carelessly down across the landscape, making its own way, setting its own standard, as suited a thing that was almost entirely an idea—abruptly forked. To the left, it twisted its way into another deep tangle of briars, each one equipped with thorns as long and viciously sharp as hatpins. To the right, it wound its way through an orchard of low, orange-leafed trees, their branches heavy with unfamiliar fruits, their roots growing with such wild abandon that they broke through the brick and turned the already-treacherous road even more so.

Avery found that he was no longer impressed by owls larger than owls had any reason to be. At least this one was a color he was accustomed to seeing on owls, and not pink, or purple, or a vivid green. The fork in the road was much more of a concern.

"Hello," said Zib, to the owl.

The Crow Girl rolled her eyes. "Ugh. Broom. What are you doing here?"

"The same as I ever am," said the owl, and it was no longer strange to hear an owl speak: clearly, that was what owls *did* in the Up-and-Under. "Warning travelers to be careful with their choices, and keeping watch over children who are out past their bedtimes. Children." The owl turned its head, regarding Avery and Zib with enormous amber eyes. If Meadowsweet's gaze had been like entering a staring contest with Halloween, this was like looking into a treasured jack-o-lantern, seeing all the wonders of a wild, wonderful night reflected in the candle's glare.

Broom's voice was soft and kind. Zib thought immediately of her father, who had never once raised his voice in anger, not even when the children on his bus were naughty beyond all reasonable measure. Avery thought of his math tutor, who always tried his best, despite Avery's hopelessness with more advanced concepts. Both of them found that they trusted the owl, which was a nice change, given how many other things they had found and failed to trust since arriving in the Up-and-Under.

"You are out past your bedtime and before your bedtime and until bedtime ceases to have any meaning whatsoever," said Broom. "Why have you done this? Why have you come here?"

"Oh shush, you flying mop," said the Crow Girl. "I have them in hand. I'll get them to the City, you watch and see."

"Are you sure that's where you're taking them?" asked Broom, his head swiveling back to face the Crow Girl.

She bristled—literally bristled, the feathers of her dress lifting and puffing out, until she looked as though she were wearing a long shirt three sizes too big for her. "We're on the improbable road!" she protested. "If I were planning to delay, betray, take them the wrong way, we wouldn't be on the *road*. The road wouldn't *let* us be."

"You might not know," said Broom, and again, his voice was gentle. He turned back to Avery and Zib. "Do you have Crow Girls where you come from?"

Silent, they shook their heads.

"Crow Girls serve two masters. They're made by the Queen of Swords, because she can't stand things that don't belong to her, but she's fickle, and she doesn't like the mischief they get up to when she's not keeping an active eye on them. So she gives them away, to someone whose name I won't say, because that person listens to the owls, that person hates and remembers us, and if she hears her name on my beak, she'll come for you for no reason other than to spite me. Even a Crow Girl who thinks she's doing the right thing can betray you because her other master tells her to."

Avery blinked slowly. Then he turned to the Crow Girl. "Is it true?" he asked.

Her feathers lost their puff and drooped, sleeking back down as she slumped. "It is," she admitted. "I didn't know. When the Queen of Swords said she could set me free, she didn't tell me there was a cage on the other end. She didn't say she'd wrap me in tangles and hand all their ends to a bad person. The Queen likes to own things. She'll make monsters of you all if we don't get you away from here. But she doesn't like to take *care* of them."

"Who do you belong to?" asked Zib.

The Crow Girl drooped further. "I can't say it," she said. "If I say it, she'll remember who I am, she'll know where I am, she'll come to collect me and carry me away, and she'll know you're here, she'll see you and she'll take you too, because *her* keeper loves new things. I hate cages. Don't make me say it."

"We won't," said Zib, and patted the Crow Girl hesitantly on the arm, the way her mother sometimes patted her. "I promise."

The Crow Girl smiled bright as anything, her distress instantly forgotten as she turned to Broom. "The road splits, and I don't know which way to go. We're looking for a lock to fit our skeleton key. Do you know the way?"

"Locks are tricky things," said Broom. "Either way could be the right one, and either way could be wrong."

"We don't have *time* for this," blurted Avery. "If the Queen of Swords is so dangerous, we need to not be here anymore. We can't stand around arguing about which way we're going!" He turned resolutely to the left branch of the path and began stomping away, his shineless shoes thudding on the bricks.

The Crow Girl stared after him, mouth hanging slightly open. Then she whirled around, grabbing Zib by the shoulders, and said, "I'll go after him. He's too delicate to go alone. Take the flying mop and go the other way. If we find the lock, I'll come find you. If you find the lock, bring it back here and wait for us. We'll have you to the Impossible City in no time!" She burst into crows before Zib could say anything, all of them flying wildly after the rapidly dwindling Avery.

Zib blinked, her hair wilting slightly as she realized what had happened. Then she turned to Broom, and said, in a meek voice, "Will you go with me?"

"No, child." Broom tucked his vast white wings against his chest, looking as sympathetic as an owl could look. "I do not belong to the Queen of Swords, but I am her subject as long as I live in her lands, and I will not go against her by helping you. The road will keep you safe. Stay on the road, and you will be protected. I hope I see you again."

Then he was gone, in a great buffeting of silent feathers, and Zib was alone.

SEVEN
THE QUEEN OF SWORDS

Zib stared at the place where the owl had been, willing herself not to cry even as hot tears prickled at her eyes, burning them. She was alone. Avery and the Crow Girl were off having an adventure without her, and even the owl wouldn't stay with her. No one ever stayed.

No one ever had. So why should this place be any different? Angrily, she swept her arm across her face, chasing the swelling tears away, and turned to stomp down the right branch of the road, into the orchard heavy with unfamiliar fruit.

Her stomach was full, and so she didn't pick any of the strange spheres, which were covered with tiny, nubby spikes, but eyed them warily. If they fell and hit her, it would probably hurt, and she didn't like being hurt. Avery was upset because he'd lost the shine from his shoes—ha! She'd lost her shoes entirely, and one sock, and was barely on the civilized side of barefoot. Zib scowled before bending down, pulling off her remaining sock, and hurling it into the bushes. Let someone else be civilized. The Crow Girl got by just fine without socks.

As soon as the sock disappeared in the weeds, she felt a pang of guilt. Her parents worked hard to buy her those socks, and she'd already lost her shoes, and her mother was always so disappointed when she came home with holes where her toes were or tears where her ankles were, and how much more disappointed would she be by an entire missing pair? It wasn't kind. Zib glanced anxiously around. She wasn't supposed to leave the road. She also wasn't supposed to be walking it all by herself, and it wasn't like there was anything around here that would hurt her; it was nothing but trees and berry bushes and weeds as far as her eye could see.

Sometimes things which seem like excellent ideas are actually terrible ones, and we wait for someone to tell us so. Sometimes, if we're lucky, that person comes along and says "stop" before it's too late.

No one came along. No one said "stop."

Zib stepped off the path.

The grass, for all that it was dry and windswept, was soft under her bare feet, and the stones seemed to roll out of the way, leaving her with nothing but gentle surfaces to walk upon. Her sock couldn't have gone far. All she had to do was find it and she'd be able to go back to the road and keep looking for the lock. Something white caught her attention. She turned, and there was her sock, hanging on a nearby bush. Triumphant, she rushed over to grab it, then ran back to the road—or ran in the direction of the road, anyway, because when she reached the place where it should have been, there was no road there at all.

Zib stopped, blinking repeatedly, trying to make sense of what she saw. The grass looked like all the grass around it. There were trees, and bushes, and no space wide enough to place a road, no space at all. The road wasn't there. The road had *never* been there.

"I got turned around, that's all," she said, and started in another direction. The road would be there. Surely the road would be there.

The road wasn't there.

Zib stopped again, expression going very solemn and small. The road had abandoned her because she had abandoned the road. She was lost. But Avery and the Crow Girl were still on the road, and the Crow Girl had left them once, to get food, and come back by looking for *them,* not the road. So all she had to do was look for her friends, and everything would be all right again.

Still clutching her sock, she turned until she thought she was facing the right direction, and began to walk.

It is one thing to walk through an unfamiliar orchard, in an unfamiliar country, when there is a road to walk upon. A road—even an improbable road—is a safe, secure thing, saying "someone wanted to go from *here* to *there,* and so they made a way to do it comfortably." It skirts the worst of the brambles and briars, the stickiest of swamps and the deepest of lakes. It protects, simply by existing. It is another thing altogether to walk through that same unfamiliar orchard, in that same unfamiliar country, when there is no road at all.

Zib walked as quickly as she dared, tripping over hidden tree roots and stepping on fallen bits of berry bush. The stones that had seemed to roll out of her way before were rolling into her way now, making every step hurt, until it felt like the soles of her feet were black with bruises. She kept walking, clutching her single sock like it was some kind of a security blanket.

When she came to the edge of the orchard, she stumbled, barely catching herself. In front of her was not the improbable road, not the open fields of berry bushes, but what looked like a part of the Tangle, only coaxed, somehow, into a glorious ballroom crafted entirely from thorny briars. The high, vaulted ceiling was open enough to let the light shine in, passing through leaves in varying shades of green and purple, until it created the illusion of stained glass. Zib knew, without even looking, that the orchard was no longer behind her: there was only the briar, going on forever.

At the center of the room of briars was a throne made of loops and tangles. On the throne was a woman, dressed in a gown of flower petals and mist, with a crown of silver filigree atop her head. Her skin was pale and almost gray, like the clouds that danced on the western wind, and her hair was long and white and free of snarls.

She was impossibly beautiful. She looked like sunshine on a Saturday, like chocolate cake and afternoons with no homework. She had a smile like a mother's praise, all sugar and softness, and Zib stared at her, wanting nothing more than to throw herself into those welcoming, unfamiliar arms.

As Zib's eyes adjusted to the gloom, she saw the shape of a sword embroidered on the front of the woman's gown. As if that were the key, more swords appeared, hidden in the filigree of the woman's crown, woven into the briars of her throne, created by the shadows on the mossy ground. But of course she was the Queen of Swords. Who else could she have been, to be so beautiful, to be so perfectly here?

If you trust her, you'll never get home, whispered a voice in the back of her mind, a voice that sounded so much like the Crow Girl that Zib nearly looked over her shoulder to see if she'd been followed. That was silly. The Crow Girl was with Avery, looking for a lock to fit their skeleton key. Avery couldn't be left alone. He was delicate.

Zib had never been allowed to be delicate. From the day she was born, she had been told to be tough, to be bold, to pick herself up and dust herself off and keep running. Sometimes she wondered what it was like, to be allowed to fall down and stay fallen.

"Hello, little girl," said the incredible woman. "What's your name?"

"Zib," said Zib.

"They call me the Queen of Swords. This is my protectorate, and I would very much like to be your friend, if you would be willing to have me." She leaned forward on her throne, smile growing wider. "We could do such wonderful things together."

Queens are cruel monsters. They eat and eat and are never full, and they leave lesser beasts in their wake, thought Zib. Still, she stepped forward, lured by the Queen's smile, so sweet, and her hands, so soft, and the idea that it would be nice to be delicate, for a change. It would be nice to be cherished, and protected, and *safe*.

Thorn briars, even enchanted thorn briars—perhaps especially enchanted thorn briars, which must on some level resent the fact that someone is telling them what to do; briars are meant to be wild, fey things, growing as wild and wide as they desire, driven by nothing but their own fickle whims—must, on occasion, drop pieces of themselves. This is how they spread, and how they cleanse themselves of debris, that they may not collapse under the weight of their own dead branches, their own unnecessary leaves. Zib took another step toward the Queen. Her bare foot, shorn of shoe and sock, clad only in dirt, which concealed but did not protect, came down squarely on a fallen bit of briar, the thorns biting deep enough to draw blood.

Zib screamed.

There is nothing quite like the earnest, full-throated

scream of a child in pain, but to dismiss Zib's scream as something so ordinary is to do it, and Zib, a great disservice. For since she was an infant, she had possessed a scream that could shake windows and wake sleeping strangers, that seemed to reach past the normal sounds and frequencies of agony and grab hold of something deeper, darker, and far more primal.

She screamed and the Queen of Swords shied away, her delicate composure broken by her confusion. "What is that *noise*?" she demanded. "Stop it at once! I command you!"

Pain had broken the Queen's thrall quite completely, and Zib did not obey. She dropped to one knee and clutched at her wounded foot instead, trying to extract the betraying briar from her flesh. The thorns were wicked. They snatched and tore at her skin as she pulled them, until she screamed again, this time less in pain and more in agonized frustration.

The Queen of Swords halfway rose from her throne, no longer smiling, no longer quite so perfect, for no one seems quite perfect when they are in a temper. "You *must* stop, or you won't be welcome here any longer!" she cried. "I'll refuse to keep you! I'll banish you from my lands!"

This was a baffling enough series of statements that Zib stopped screaming and simply blinked at the Queen of Swords. Even her hair seemed to echo the question in her eyes, curling around her face in a vast cloud of confusion. Finally, she asked, "Is that meant to be a threat?"

"Yes! All the best things are here! This is the protectorate of winds and transformation, of spades and changes! My gales are the best gales, my storms the best storms, and you'll have none of them, *none,* if you can't stop making that horrific noise!"

Zib stood, slowly. "I'm looking for a lock to fit a skeleton key. I'm walking the improbable road to the Impossible City with my friends, and we want to be gone. Tell me how to find the lock and how to get back on the road, and I'll leave, and you'll never have to see me again."

The Queen of Swords scowled at her. She was still beautiful. It is a myth that goodness is always lovely and wickedness is always dreadful to behold; the people who say such things have reason for their claims and would rather those reasons not be overly explored. But she was far less compelling without a sweet smile curving her lips and a delicate angle canting her chin. A hurricane can be beautiful. That doesn't mean it would be a good idea to go dancing with one simply because it asked you.

Zib smiled, sweet as sugar candy, and opened her mouth, and screamed again.

The Queen of Swords clapped her hands over her ears. "Enough, *enough*!" she cried. "Stop that noise and you can have your lock, and take it with you out of my protectorate as fast as feet can carry you! I need beasts and better, not filthy, screaming children!"

Avery would have been hurt by her words. Avery didn't think of himself as "filthy," would have been shocked and horrified to realize that the label was closer to true than not. He was not a child built for mud puddles and brambles, and there was nothing wrong with that, for every child is built differently, and meant for different things. For example, to Zib, the word "filthy" was a simple statement of fact, neither cruel nor a reason to be ashamed.

"I took a bath just yesterday," she said brightly, and held out her hands.

The Queen of Swords, nose wrinkled in disgust, reached into the shimmering folds of her gown and pulled out a padlock carved from a single solid piece of stone. Zib pulled the bit of bramble from her foot and walked closer. The Queen's lip curled, but she placed the lock in Zib's hands.

It was heavy, and cold, and exactly what they needed. Zib closed her eyes.

"It's *improbable* that I found the Queen of Swords by accident," she said, even though it was nothing of the sort, for the Queen had surely been seeking them since their arrival. "It's *improbable* that she had the lock we needed, and it's *improbable* that me screaming would be enough to get it."

She cracked an eye open. There, glimmering dimly through the muddy ground, was a brick, and where there was one brick, there was another, until she could see the improbable road stretching out before her like a promise of something better yet to come.

Opening both eyes, Zib turned and curtseyed to the Queen of Swords. Yes, the woman might be wicked, and yes, Zib had been well warned that Queens were fabulous monsters, but that was no cause to be rude.

"Thank you for the lock," she said. "I'll find my friends and we'll go, quick as anything. You won't have to worry about us anymore." Then she turned and walked quickly away, her wounded foot leaving smears of blood on the glittering bricks as she went. The Queen watched her with resentment and respect, for it had been a long time since she'd been denied something she truly wanted to have—but that, it should be said, is another story.

Zib clutched the lock to her chest as she walked, moving faster and faster through the shadows beneath the brambles, until finally she was running, running as fast as she could, leaves and tangled branches flashing all around her. She was still running when the brambles came to an abrupt end, and she found herself racing down the stretch of the improbable road that ran between the berry bushes, where they had first arrived. She knew that if she looked back, she would see the Tangle, and so she didn't bother looking.

An adult might have bitten and worried at the question of how the land had twisted itself beneath her feet, chewing at the contradictions like a dog chews at a flea. Zib was still a child, and she accepted the change with simple gratitude. If anything, this way of doing things simply made more sense than going the long way every time you needed to get somewhere. Why, if the roads could bend to suit every person's needs, there wouldn't be any reason not to spend every weekend with her grandparents by the sea, and wouldn't that be a marvelous thing?

So Zib ran, and ran, as a white owl circled approvingly overhead, as the Queen of Swords sat and brooded in her bower of briars, until two figures appeared on the road ahead of her. She found the strength to run even faster then, and raced along the road with the lock clasped tight, stopping when she reached them.

The Crow Girl blinked, once. Avery, on the other hand, looked bewildered—and alarmed. Unlike Zib, he did not like it when things he thought to be rules were broken.

"How are you here? You should be somewhere else," he said.

"The road moved," she said. "I have the lock."

"Let me see," said the Crow Girl. Zib solemnly surrendered her prize. The Crow Girl turned it over and over, studying it thoughtfully, before she broke into the biggest, brightest smile either of them had seen from her. "It's a skeleton lock, all right! We can go right to the protectorate of the Queen of Wands and not have to meet the King of Cups at all. Where did you find it?"

"The Queen of Swords gave it to me if I would promise to stop screaming and leave as quickly as possible," said Zib.

Avery stared. The Crow Girl beamed.

"Clever, clever, and no mistake of *that*! Come, come, come." She started walking toward the nearest tree, lock in hand. "We have to hang it high if it's to work, but not so high the key can't reach. Challenge, not impossibility, you see?"

"No," said Avery. Then: "I thought we were supposed to be afraid of the Queen of Swords."

"She was very beautiful, and very frightening," said Zib. "I don't think I liked her." But she had almost gone to her all the same, hadn't she? Another few steps and Zib's part in the story would have ended. This would have become Avery's story, and Avery's alone, the brave little boy who climbed over a wall and found a friend and lost the friend and learned important life lessons before returning home sadder, wiser, and better prepared to become an adult, with adult thoughts and adult concerns. It was an unsettling thought. Even more unsettling was that the shape of it felt true and right and dangerously close, like so many stories had been told that way that this story *wanted* to be rid of her, to narrow itself to one child, one destination, one destiny.

It wasn't right or fair, that stories should play favorites like that. Zib decided, then and there, that she would see this one all the way to the end: she wouldn't be shaken off. No matter what, she wouldn't let go of what was hers.

The Crow Girl ignored them both as she reached up and hung the lock on a high branch, not so high as to be outside her reach, but very nearly. Then she stepped back, cocking her head this way and that before she reached up and adjusted the angle of the lock, ever so slightly, tilting it toward the brambles.

"There," she said. "All we have to do now is open it."

The tree shivered. The tree shook. The tree stretched upward, until the lock was well above any of their heads, placed impossibly high.

Avery gaped at it. "Trees aren't supposed to *move*," he said. "Now no one can reach the lock."

"I can!" Zib snatched the skeleton key from his hand before he could protest. She ran for the tree, flinging herself into its lowest branches like she trusted them, implicitly, to catch her—and they did, they did, they cradled her close, holding her like she was the most precious thing in this or any other world. Her bare feet found easy purchase on the bark, and her hands traded the key between them, now here, now there, as she grabbed and pulled and climbed higher and higher and higher still, until she was on the branch where the lock hung, silent and closed, until she was inching toward it with the key still in her grasp.

She reached down and slid the key easily into place. Avery held his breath. She turned the key in the lock, and there was a sharp clicking sound, and the hasp fell open, and the lock fell away from the tree, tumbling into the hole that had opened where the ground should have been.

"Here we go!" shouted the Crow Girl. She grabbed hold of Avery, having long since figured out that some things were easier for him, and better, if he had help, and dove into the hole, carrying him with her. He screamed, once, as they plummeted down into the misty depths, and then they were gone.

"Whee!" shouted Zib, and swung herself away from the branch, dangling for a moment before she let go and fell after them.

The hole closed once she was through it. Overhead, the white owl watched, and whatever he thought, he did not say.

EIGHT
IN THE HOLE

They fell quickly through what felt like a layer of mist or fog, something cool and clammy that chilled the skin and saturated the clothing, leaving all of them damp and somewhat bedraggled. Avery screamed. Zib shrieked, which is not the same thing at all. The Crow Girl laughed and laughed, a sound that was suspiciously like the cawing of a flock of birds, and kept hold of Avery, who might well have found his way to a bad end if permitted to fall without someone holding on to him.

They were in a tunnel, that much was plain, for their fall brought them periodically into contact with one wall or another, bouncing back and forth like balls in a machine. Finally, their backs settled into a groove that seemed to have been carved for that very purpose, for it was smooth and polished, like a playground slide made of ice or chilled granite. Zib's hair grabbed at the stone, in its usual, uncivilized manner, until several strands were pulled out and left behind, and the rest of her hair retreated to the safer tangles near her head. Avery howled, slapping the Crow Girl several times in his panic, so that she lost her grip on him and fell away. Almost immediately, Zib's hand found his in the darkness, and they held each other tightly, not letting go.

Down and down and down they fell, until the air thickened into fog around them once more and their fall became a plummet, the slide vanishing from beneath their bodies, replaced by nothing but empty air. The Crow Girl gasped and burst into birds. Zib's shrieks of delight became a howl of fear. Avery screamed harder.

Two children struck the surface of the freezing water, hard enough to force their bodies some distance below the surface, into the depths. The crows circled above it, cawing panic, even as the fog began to clear, revealing the snowcapped peaks of jagged mountains that jutted from the earth like the claws of some forgotten beast.

A girl stood on the shore, looking at the water with solemn eyes. The crows landed all around her, cawing frantically.

"Well, yes, I *can*," said the girl. "But if I do, it will certainly attract attention, and I'll need you to go and see what comes on the mountain roads. Can you do that?"

The crows cawed assent and rose into the air, dispersing in all directions, until it was as if they had never been there at all. The girl watched them go for a moment. Then she walked into the water, never flinching at the chill. She did not swim; the water offered no resistance. She simply strolled, like the improbable road was somehow rising up to meet her.

Avery and Zib, having crashed together and grabbed hold as they fell, were still holding tight to one another's hands. This made it difficult for them to swim, and both of them knew, without being able to say anything about it, that they would have been better off letting go. It is difficult to swim when suddenly dropped from a great height into a dark, icy lake. The shock alone is more than the body wants to bear. It is even more difficult to do so when holding on to someone else's hand, however beloved they may be. Avery and Zib had not yet found their way to loving one another, but they had more than found their way to the fear of being in this strange new world alone, and so they held on and tried to swim at the same time, deep and drowning and afraid.

When hands grasped the collars of their shirts, both stiffened but did not try to break away. Avery assumed it was the Crow Girl, come to save them once again, as she had in the mudslide. Zib assumed it was the Queen of Swords, having changed her mind about the shrillness of Zib's screaming. Either way, it would get them out of the water, and so they stopped fighting, stopped thrashing, and let themselves be pulled from the depths.

The girl walked out of the water as easily as she had walked in, dragging the two children with her. When they were safely free of the lake, she let them go, and they collapsed, coughing and wheezing and spitting up water, while she watched from a polite distance.

Avery was the first to recover. He was very fond of baths, and laundry, and anything else that left him clean, after all, and while the lake had been colder than a winter bath, he was young and inclined to briskness. He spat out the last traces of lake water and clambered to his feet, wiping wet hands on wet trousers before turning to offer Zib his hands.

Zib, it should be said, was much the worse for wear. She was not as fond of baths, or cleanliness, as Avery was; viewed them, for the most part, as necessary evils. Her hair was matted down against her head, as heavy with water as a sponge, and her skirt clung to her legs like the scales of a mermaid. She took Avery's hands despite that, letting him pull her to her feet, wobbling and leaning against him for the strength she no longer seemed to have.

"Where's the Crow Girl?" she asked, glancing to the lake with some alarm. She was cold and she was tired and she wasn't sure she'd ever see the surface again if she dove in even one more time.

"She went to scout the mountain roads," said an unfamiliar voice.

Zib and Avery turned.

The girl was very pale, with waterweeds in her hair and tangled around her toes. Her feet were bare, and all of her glistened with a silvery sheen, like she had been dusted in glitter and set out into the world to see what could be seen.

"Who are you?" asked Avery.

"*What* are you?" asked Zib, forgetting her manners in the face of her awe. Avery stuck an elbow in her side, but it was too late: the question had been asked.

"My name is Niamh," said the girl. "I pulled you out of the water. I come from a city deep beneath the surface of a lake, in a place so cold that the ice only thaws once every hundred years."

"People don't live under lakes," said Avery. "There's no air. Only water. People don't breathe water."

"Oh, but you see, the people where I'm from don't breathe at all." Niamh smiled, showing teeth like pearls. "And only when the ice melts do we come up to the surface to see how other people live. But while I was on the shore gathering stones, a storm came, and the Page of Frozen Waters appeared, and snatched me up, and carried me to the King of Cups. He's a very cruel king, and he kept me for so long that the ice froze solid again, and now I'm just a drowned girl with no city at all, until the next time the thaw comes."

"A hundred years is a very long while," said Avery. He couldn't let himself think too hard about the way her skin glistened, or her claims to come from a place where people didn't breathe. Surely she was kidding. "Won't you be too old then to swim?"

"Not at all. When I'm home, I don't breathe, and when I'm here, I don't age. That way, I can always make it back to the ice, if I'm clever."

Zib, though, had what felt like a more important question. "Who is the Page of Frozen Waters?"

Niamh sobered. "She is the worst of all the King's subjects, because she loves him and hates him at the same time, and would do anything to please him. She commands the crows, and they do her bidding. For him, she gathers every strange thing that comes into the Up-and-Under, even stealing them from under the nose of the Queen of Swords, who is wicked in her own way, but never so much as the King of Cups. The Page will gather you, if you're not careful."

Avery and Zib exchanged a glance and stepped closer together, suddenly afraid of this glittering girl, and of everything her presence might entail.

Avery thought of the Crow Girl, of her promise that the skeleton key and its lock would allow them to pass over the protectorate of the King of Cups without attracting his attention. But here they were, soaked and cold and on their own, and he knew—*knew*—that they hadn't passed over the King's protectorate at all. They had fallen right down into the middle of it, and the Crow Girl had vanished.

Zib thought of the Crow Girl as well, but she thought of the way the girl had tried to help them, the way she had broken into birds and fled, the way she had balked at the idea of control by kings or queens of any kind. The Page of Frozen Waters must have been her greatest nightmare, and if she never came back, Zib didn't know if she'd be able to blame her, and if she never came back, Zib didn't know if she'd be able to forgive her, either. It was all so complicated, and she was cold. So cold.

Niamh looked at the shivering children with sympathy. She looked somewhat younger than they were, yes, but she was a daughter of the city beneath the lake, the city that had—that needed—no name, for how many spectacular cities of shell and silver could one world contain? She was old enough to have seen so many stories spin themselves across the shore, and she was sorry to see children suffer.

"Come with me," she said. "Your Crow Girl will find us, if she's free to do so, or not find us, if the Page of Frozen Waters has seized hold of her, for the Page trades cleverness for cruelty, and rarely remembers to ask the proper questions. I can make a fire. You can get warm and dry and decide what happens next."

"Won't you melt?" blurted Zib.

Niamh smiled. "I come from the ice, but I'm not ice. You come from the earth, but you're not earth. You don't melt to mud in water, and I don't melt when confronted by fire. Although . . ." She leaned forward, squinting at the two of them. "Maybe you don't *both* come from earth. There's something mismatched about you. There could be other elements."

"We come from the same town," said Avery, and took Zib's hand, and held it stubbornly tight, a challenging expression on his face.

The glittering girl didn't argue. She simply nodded, and said, "Follow me," as she turned to walk back the way she had come, back into the crevasse which gaped, silent and crystalline, in the mountain's side.

Before the wall, before the mudslide and the tunnel

of mist, before the girls who came from crows and the owls that talked, Avery and Zib might have stayed where they were, watching the stranger dwindle in the distance. They might have chosen to run, to seek other ways of warming themselves, for they were both reasonably cautious children with no interest in breaking their parents' hearts. But they were cold, and they were wet, and the Up-and-Under had a way of wearing such kinds of caution away, a little bit at a time, replacing them with curiosity and the quiet conviction that sometimes, the right thing was to follow.

So they followed.

The air inside of the crevasse was even colder than the air outside. It bit and stung their skins, until Avery looked over his shoulder, clearly thinking of going back. The opening had disappeared in a fog of ice and cold, and he could no longer be sure that it existed. The only way out was forward, following Niamh. The thought that this could be a terrible trap occurred to him, and was quickly denied. That sort of thinking would do him no good and might do him a great deal of ill. He glanced at Zib.

Her clothing was still soaked, but her hair seemed to have wrung itself out, once again rising in a glorious and terrible tangle, as frizzy and unconfined as ever. It was a relief, of a kind, to see her hair so defiant of gravity, and wetness, and a dozen other forces he didn't have a name for. As long as her hair was alert, she was still Zib, and as long as she was still Zib, he was still Avery, and they could make it through this. They could.

The tunnel around them widened out abruptly enough to be disorienting, and they were suddenly standing on a clear patch of earth, dotted with scrubby flowers and low berry plants that looked something like strawberries, and something like basil, and something like nothing he had ever seen before. Niamh was already in motion, gathering twigs and branches from the stretch of ground against the cliff face and piling them into a heap in the center of the clear space.

Straight rock walls defined the space on two sides, like a folded piece of paper standing on a table. A swift-moving river defined it on the third, rushing to fall down, down, down, in a cascade of falling water and hissing foam. The fourth side was nothingness, the land dropping away to provide the waterfall something to fall over, the clouds someplace to hang. What was below those clouds could not be seen, for they were too dense, too clustered together. It could have been the end of the world, for all that he could see.

"I'm getting tired of cliffs," said Avery, and turned, and looked up at what seemed to be the tallest, sheerest stretch of rock he had ever seen. Trees grew all along the top; one dropped a branch as he watched, and Niamh was quick to dart over and retrieve it. "What's at the top?"

"The protectorate of the Queen of Swords," said Niamh. "She and the King of Cups are unhappy neighbors, both quite sure the other is planning something. Although, I suppose it should be said, neither of them is *wrong*. They are both terrible people."

"That seems like an unkind way to speak of your

king," said Avery, who had never had a king of his own, but assumed they were something like teachers, or fathers, in the amount of respect they were expected to receive.

"He is an unkind king, at best, and besides, he isn't mine," said Niamh. "The city beneath the lake is its own protectorate, and we answer to no king, having decided that ours was more useful as an eel many centuries ago."

"An eel?" asked Zib.

"He's very happy this way, and as he makes fewer proclamations, so are we." Niamh held her hands above the pile of wood, which burst into vigorous flame. Zib made a small sound of wordless joy and ran to warm herself. Avery followed, more slowly.

"How did you do that?" he asked. "I thought you said you came from the ice."

"Yes," said Niamh. "I took the cold away from the wood, so all it had left was heat, and heat wants to be fire more than anything else in the world, so when it had the opportunity, it was very happy to burn. When you take something away, there's room for everything that's left to be bigger, if it wants to."

Avery wanted to argue with this, but he couldn't find the words. He joined Zib next to the fire. The warmth was good, as long as he didn't stand close enough for it to burn him.

Zib was not so careful. Her clothes steamed with escaping lake water; her hair crisped and danced back from the flame, barely escaping being singed. It was offensive, almost, how careless she was being, when he needed her to get home.

Anger bubbled up in his chest, hot and poisonous. Sometimes anger is a good, true thing, because the world is so often unfair, and unfairness deserves to be acknowledged. But all too often, anger is another feeling in its Sunday clothes, sadness or envy or—most dangerous of all—fear. Avery was afraid of losing Zib. He was afraid of being alone in this strange place, and most of all, he was afraid of never going home. All that fear swirled together, until it hung around his heart like a shroud, weighing it down, turning furious and foul.

She reached out, like she was going to touch the flame with her naked hand. Something inside him snapped.

"Stop that!" he shouted, and pushed her, away from the fire, toward the edge of the drop-off. "You keep *doing* that! You keep acting like it doesn't matter if something happens to you, but it does matter, it *does,* because if something happens to you, I don't get to go home, ever! Stupid! Selfish!"

Niamh, who was older than she looked, watched with solemn, grieving eyes, for she knew that the words Avery hurled at Zib like knives were the words that he was secretly hurling at himself, the words that stabbed deep into his heart and opened wounds that nothing but time would ever start to heal. She did not yet know these children well enough to feel as if she were allowed to intervene, but could only wait, and watch, and hope that they would find their way to peace without outside assistance.

Zib stumbled back, horror and confusion on her

face. Her hair drooped, weighted down with dismay. "What are you . . . what are you talking about?" she stammered. "I only wanted to be warm! I didn't do anything wrong!"

Avery could have answered her. Could have said that he was afraid, that he didn't want her to risk herself because he didn't know what he would do without her. Could have told her all manner of things, true things, things that she needed to hear, things that would, by coming out into the open, have made them both better.

He pushed her again.

Zib stared at him, eyes gone huge and mouth gone small. Then she shuddered, like she was shaking away the clinging film of a particularly unpleasant dream, and stood up as straight as she could. She would have been taller than him even without her hair. With it, she towered, and he felt small, and ashamed, and backed away.

"Fine," she said. "I don't know why I thought you'd be my friend, anyway. You're mean and you're selfish and you're . . . you're *narrow*. You look at things and you think you're the only one who knows what they're supposed to be and that anyone who thinks different from you is wrong, wrong, wrong. But maybe you're wrong. Did you ever think of that? Maybe all the people telling you it's a forest are the ones who're right, and you're the only one insisting that it's nothing but a tree! I don't want to be your friend. I don't want to do anything with you. I wish I weren't anywhere *near* you!"

Someone laughed. It was a bright, merry sound, like

the pealing of bells from a carousel calliope as it started to move, or the gossiping of birds on the first day of spring. It should have been a sweet sound—but there was something poisonous to it, something rotten. It was the twitter of a bird about to ram its beak through a toad's skull, or the ringing of a bell attached to a carousel damaged by fire. It was wrong, and it was wicked, and it was oh so very close.

The woman who stepped out of the fog—stepped out of the empty air, where nothing but clouds should have been light enough to stay suspended—looked to be of an age with the high school girls Avery sometimes saw walking home in the first light of evening, their shirts pressed and their skirts prim and their books carried exactly so. She was tall, slim, straight as an arrow, with a long, graceful neck and the carriage of a bird of prey, smooth and assured in every motion. Her hair was the color of charcoal, bound back in an elaborate braid studded with chunks of polished glass. Her eyes were the color of the fog around her, and she was dressed like a dancer, in smooth gray hose and a belted tunic that seemed archaic and accurate at the same time. Someone like her could never have dressed any other way.

Niamh took a step backward, her eyes going wide. She raised her hands in front of her in a warding gesture. "Quickly, both of you, come here," she said, and her voice was tight with fear. "It will be all right, but you must come now."

"Who is she?" asked Avery, and took two stumbling steps back, toward the drowned girl.

Perhaps that was what saved him. Or perhaps Zib had already been lost, had been lost the moment her careless words summoned this specter out of the fog. It can be so difficult to tell, even with the graces of hindsight, which shows all but forgives nothing.

The woman settled her feet on the cliff, blew Avery a kiss, and said, "Why, I am the Page of Frozen Waters, of course, and everything here belongs to my lord and master, which means everything here belongs to me, which means you should be grateful that the toll is tiny as it is. A mere token, really. Nothing of concern."

Zib, seeming to suddenly realize that the Page was standing between her and her friends, tried to run forward. The Page spun on one booted heel and planted her hands on Zib's shoulders, pushing her easily back, so that her bare feet lost traction on the stone, so that she was standing on nothing at all. Zib was no Page of Frozen Waters, to dance on fog and clouds. She was as simple and solid as any child who has ever climbed trees, or hunted frogs through mud puddles, or refused to brush her hair. She fell without a sound, eyes wide and solemn, hands reaching for the help they could not grasp.

The Page of Frozen Waters turned back to Avery and Niamh. She bowed mockingly, a sweet smile on her face as she straightened. "I thank you, and my lord thanks you, and her bones may dream a thousand years in the rocks at the bottom, or they may not, and it's none of your concern either way."

"It *is* my concern!" Avery ran toward her, past the fire, hands outstretched, and for one terrible moment, it seemed as if he might push the Page of Frozen Waters after Zib, might have his revenge in one terrible, irrevocable gesture. Instead, he grabbed the front of her tunic and yanked her toward him, shouting, "You go bring her back! You bring her back *right now*!"

"Oh, you want the little thing now? That's not what I heard before. It seemed to me that I was doing you a favor." The Page of Frozen Waters crouched down until their eyes were level. She was smiling again, but there was nothing of sweetness in her now. "Are you saying I was wrong?"

"Don't touch him," said Niamh, and came no closer.

"He touched me first, child; that means your protection is over." The Page of Frozen Waters kept her eyes on Avery. "Are you saying I was wrong?" she repeated.

"Yes," he whispered.

"Then I suppose a reunion is in order." She leaned closer, closer still, and whispered, next to his ear, "You'll find her at the bottom, if you're fortunate enough to find her at all." Then she straightened, grabbing him by the arm and spinning him around as she did, so that he teetered on the edge of the abyss.

"Goodbye," she said, and pushed him over. He screamed as he fell. She glanced back to Niamh, winked, and stepped into the empty air, plummeting quickly out of sight.

Niamh stood on the other side of the fire, clutching her gown above her heart, tears springing to her eyes and freezing there, so that they fell like silent diamonds to the ground at her feet. She was still standing there, weeping, when a murder of crows dropped from the sky and pieced itself together in front of her, a puzzle happening in the blink of an eye, and became the familiar shape of the Crow Girl.

The Crow Girl looked around, and frowned. "Where are they?" she asked, looking to Niamh. "Where are the children?"

But Niamh could only cry.

NINE

THE PAGE OF
FROZEN WATERS

There are many different kinds of falling, as many different kinds of falling as there are opportunities to fall. There is falling through earth, surrounded by mud, with something to hold you up and keep you from harm. There is falling through water, through mist and ice, with something soft at the end to render the landing gentle, if not quite safe. There is falling through fire, which is painful but mercifully short. And then there is falling through nothing at all. Air is a necessary part of life on land. Air fills our lungs and steers our steps, gentle winds pushing us where we are meant to go. But air cannot stop a fall without something to fill, and Zib dropped through the layers of cloud like a stone, unable to slow herself, unable to see where she was going.

Perhaps I will land in another lake, with another drowned girl to pull me to safety, she thought, and knew it for a lie, but held it tightly all the same, for there was nothing else to do. The wind whipped her tears away as fast as they could fall, and there was no one coming to save her. No one at all.

She fell, and she fell, and it seemed that she must fall forever, that she would grow old and die still in the process of falling. It was almost a comforting thought, given the alternative, and so she closed her eyes and let the falling have her.

"Hello, child," said a voice. "What are you doing here? You don't appear to be a bird, although of course, I have been wrong before. So many people are birds and never realize it, and so many birds are people and never know, that I suppose a child might decide to fly away, if given proper incentive."

Zib cracked open one eye. The other followed, and she stared.

The owl which circled her now was the largest she had yet seen, larger than Meadowsweet, with her blue feathers, and larger than Broom, with his white feathers. This owl was all shades of red, from deepest crimson to palest pink, and had eyes as orange as any autumn leaf, and she could not say if it was male or female, nor see any reason for it to matter. An owl this large could be whatever it liked, and no one would dare to tell it no.

"Please," she said, and the wind ripped her words away, turning them into a sob, into a gasp, into a shadow of themselves. "Please, owl, won't you help me? I'm not a bird, and I'm falling, and I'm afraid."

"My name is Oak," said the owl. "If you're not a bird, why are you here? This isn't where a child belongs."

The owl sounded so puzzled, and so caring, that Zib's last frayed scrap of calm came apart, and she began to sob. She was still sobbing when the owl moved, so that she drifted down into the thick blanket of its feathers, so that its wings bore her up and slowed her descent. It smelled, not of a downy comforter or of the wild woods, but of roses, countless roses, sweet and comforting. Zib's tears slowed as she breathed in the scent of the owl's feathers, which were so strangely familiar that she found she could no longer be sad.

"Please, Oak," she said. "Can you take me back to the top? My friends are there, and they must be concerned for me."

"I wish I could," said the owl, and there was genuine regret in its voice. "But even as large as I am, you are heavy, and I can slow your fall but cannot lift you up. I will take you safely to the bottom, and perhaps there, you can find a way to climb to where your friends are waiting."

Zib wanted to argue, but knew that help, even when offered, could be snatched away from the ungrateful, and had no desire to resume her uncontrolled plummet. She held tightly to Oak's feathers instead, and together they spiraled down, down, down through the mist and the fog and the clouds, until they reached a crystalline river running through a channel of glittering stone. Oak settled to the ground, spreading its wings slightly, so that she might dismount.

The ground was slippery with spray from the river. Zib's bare feet gripped it easily. She looked at Oak, hands clasped in front of herself, hair wilder than ever after her fall.

"If there's ever anything I can do for you, I'll do it, and gladly," she said. "You've saved me, and I won't forget you."

Oak raised one massive talon and scratched at the flat disk of its face, where the feathers were lightest, pink trending into cream. "The parliament of owls will remember this offer," it said. "One night, perhaps, you'll hear us calling, and you will know your debt is due. Only stay safe until that hour, for we can collect no payment from a dead girl, nor wring any blood from a stone."

"I will," said Zib.

Oak bobbed once, as if bowing to her. Then it launched itself into the sky on silent wings and vanished into the mist, there and gone in the span of a second, and Zib was alone on the shore.

Far above her, in the concealing layers of the fog and all without her knowledge, Avery was still falling. He had tucked himself into a ball, as if for his own protection, and while his arms were perhaps less likely to be broken, and his legs less likely to strike some unexpected protrusion, he had also made himself small and comfortably compact, and so was falling faster than anything large and sprawling. Unfortunately for him, he had not considered this, being too afraid to do anything but hug his own knees and hope against all logic to land safely.

I shouldn't be here, he thought. *I should be in class, I should be home, I should be somewhere safe and reasonable and ordinary.*

Ordinary. He remembered what it was to be ordinary, to have shoes that shined and friends who knew him, who didn't try to lead him on wild adventures for the sake of seeing something new. He fumbled to pull the ruler from his pocket, suddenly thinking that he needed to hold something he could understand. Its edges bit into his palm, and it brought him no comfort. Furious, he uncurled enough to stab it away from him, into the fog.

There was no way this would be enough to save him; physics said *no,* gravity said *impossible,* probability said *forbidden.* And perhaps those truths were, more than anything else, the reasons that Avery's ruler found, not empty air, but the side of the cliff, and the angle at which it struck was such that it slid between two stones and stuck there, pulling Avery up short as it jammed into the mountain. Avery gasped, scrambling to keep his grasp on the ruler, and hung, still bouncing slightly up and down. Once he had his breath back, he reached out with his free hand and found the cliff, scrabbling until he wedged his fingers into another crack.

"Help," he said softly, and then, with more strength, "Help!" That was the skeleton key that unlocked his voice, and he began to howl, shouting, "Help! *Help!*" over and over again, until the entire valley rang with the sound of his fear.

A crow dropped down, through the fog, and landed on the ruler. "Caw," it said, cocking its head to the side and considering him carefully.

"Are you . . . are you the Crow Girl?" he gasped.

"Caw."

"She pushed me. She pushed me and I fell. Can you help me?"

"Caw," said the crow again, and took off, flying away into the fog.

Avery dangled from his ruler—which was a sturdy, faithful tool but had never been intended to support the full weight of a boy, however small—and wondered how long it would be before he was falling again. Would it hurt less, because he had stopped it for a little while? Or would it hurt more, because now he would have to begin the whole process over again? The shock, the realization that no one was coming to catch him, the dawning comprehension that just because he had fallen twice and been saved both times didn't mean he'd be saved a third time, no matter how much he wanted to be?

He would have said that falling was the worst thing that had ever happened to him, if not for the slow bruise blossoming on his heart, the bruise with Zib's wide, unhappy eyes looking back at him in the moment before she'd fallen out of view. He wanted to survive, yes, he wanted to go home, but he didn't want to do it at the expense of the people he was coming to care about.

He didn't want Zib to be gone. He certainly didn't want her to be gone believing that he hated her. This was his fault, this was all his fault, and he didn't know how to fix it.

The air grew colder around him. He felt his fingers starting to slip. Avery strained to keep hold of the ruler, afraid of what might be waiting in the fog below.

"Let go."

Avery looked wildly around. "Niamh?"

"Trust me," she said. "Let go."

Avery did not want to let go. Avery thought he would rather dangle forever than let go, even a little. But Zib was gone, and it was all his fault; if he couldn't start trusting the people who were left, he was going to fall, just like she did.

Avery let go.

His fall was short, and stopped when he struck something cold and solid and slippery, landing on his bottom. He tried to stand up, and his feet slid out from under him, leaving him seated. Niamh turned to offer him a slight, strained smile. Her hands were raised, and her hair was billowing around her like a wave, even though there was no wind to stir it.

"Don't worry," she said. "This is perfectly safe. Just try to enjoy it."

"Enjoy what?" he asked.

Niamh's smile grew. She didn't answer, only sat down on the slippery surface. crows flew out of the fog, roosting all over the two of them, covering them in warm, feathery bodies. Avery looked wildly around, trying to understand what was happening. The crows began flapping their wings, and Avery and Niamh began inching along the surface—ice, it was *ice,* they were sitting on a long ribbon of ice that curved and twisted like a carnival slide—until the force of the dozens and dozens of flapping wings became enough to propel them along at a greater and greater speed. They slid down the icy ribbon like they were sitting on polished sleds, fast and graceful and secure, Avery's shriek of dismay accompanying them all the way down.

The ice slide ended at the bottom of the cliffs, dumping them onto the frozen, stony ground. Avery scrambled to his feet, shedding crows in all directions, and looked frantically around. There was nothing but stone, glittering quartz and shimmering opal and a dozen shades of topaz, creating a cruel rainbow of cold. The crows began to spiral together, reforming themselves into the body of the Crow Girl. Niamh sat on a large quartz boulder, head bowed and shoulders shaking, trying to catch her breath. The tips of her fingers and toes were blue from the strain of spinning a ribbon of ice all the way down into the chasm.

Avery barely noticed any of this. He had yet to even realize that his ruler had been lost, left wedged into the cliffs high above. He was spinning in place, scanning the shore. Zib—stupid Zib, who thought she knew everything—was supposed to be somewhere around here. That's what the Page of Frozen Waters had said, before pushing him over the waterfall. He needed to find Zib. He needed to tell her he was sorry.

She wasn't there.

"Where is she?" he asked, barely aware that his voice was raising into a wail. A hand touched his shoulder. He stopped, and turned, and looked into the solemn, avian eyes of the Crow Girl.

"You came together, and you won't find an ending alone," she said, and her voice was soft, and sad, and more serious than he had ever heard her. "That doesn't mean you can't have all the middle your heart can hold. You don't have to stay here. You don't have to follow her. The Page of Frozen Waters has her now, and you won't get her back the way you lost her. Endings are tricky things. Remember, I told you that, when we'd barely met at all. Endings don't forgive. So have a middle. Let her go."

Avery gaped at her. "How can you *say* that?"

"I lied to you." The Crow Girl looked at him gravely. "I told you the Queen of Swords made me, the same way as she made the Bumble Bear, and I lied, because what's true isn't always what's right. She didn't make me. She broke the chains that were on me, and I told her I'd be loyal, because every caged thing wants to be loyal to the one who lets it out, but she didn't make me. I went to *her* willing. I didn't go to *him* willing."

"The Page of Frozen Waters commands the crows," said Niamh. Avery, who had almost forgotten she was there, turned to look at her. All her attention was for the Crow Girl. "She tells them where to go and what to do, and they serve as her eyes and her spies, all across the Up-and-Under. Are you spying for her still?"

"No," whispered the Crow Girl. "Not for days and days and days, not since before the Queen of Wands went—" Her eyes widened and she clapped her hands over her mouth, like she could somehow cram the words back inside.

"Since the Queen of Wands went where?" asked Avery.

The Crow Girl lowered her hands. "Missing," she said miserably. "Since the Queen of Wands went missing. Everyone blamed everyone else, and the King of Cups told the Page of Frozen Waters to see what she could see, and so she let the crows fly, she let us all fly, and not all of us . . . not all of us came back. Some were eaten, yes, and some were lost, and some found another way."

"The Queen of Swords," said Niamh.

The Crow Girl nodded. "She can cut old bonds. She cut me free, and all she asked was that I stay and serve her, be a crow in her court, and not in anybody else's. But I was and am and will be a crow still, because some things can't be taken back, and so she doesn't mind when I join children on quests, or steal fruit from her orchards. It's having me, not taming me, that matters. I'm had, I truly am."

"But where's Zib?" asked Avery. "She's not with the Queen of Wands. She's lost and she fell and no one made an ice slide to catch her, she didn't have a ruler to break her fall. She could be hurt. We have to find her."

"No one has to do anything," said the Crow Girl. "You could learn how to be happy without her, I know you could."

Avery blinked at her slowly, like her words made no sense at all. Of course he could be happy without Zib. He wasn't entirely sure he knew how to be happy *with* her. They'd only been together since the wall, and most of their time in the Up-and-Under had been strange and frightening and not what he'd call "happy" at all. Zib wasn't where his happiness was harbored.

But she was his friend, still, and she'd gone out of her way to help him, even when he hadn't been very nice to her, even when it would have been easier for her to walk away. *She* could be happy here in the Up-and-Under, where things only made as much sense as they absolutely had to, where beasts could talk and fruit could taste like anything it wanted. Maybe if they couldn't be happy together, they could be unhappy together, and maybe . . . maybe that was just as good. As long as they weren't alone.

"It doesn't matter whether I'm happy or not," he said. "I have to find her."

The Crow Girl shivered, shaking herself so that the feathers of her dress and in her hair puffed out. It should have looked silly. Somehow, it just looked scared. "Then I'll help you," she said.

"I won't," said Niamh. They both turned. The drowned girl looked at them with weary eyes, spreading her empty hands in front of herself. "I can't. The Page of Frozen Waters is there, and all my ice can't touch her, because there's nothing in her left to freeze. She'll catch me again, catch me and cage me, and this time, I won't be able to get away. I'll mark the path from the king's protectorate back to the improbable road, and I'll wait for you there, but I won't help you. Please don't ask that of me."

"I won't," said Avery, who knew what it was to be afraid. "Only be safe, if you can, and we'll see you when all this is over. All three of us will see you."

"I wish you well," said Niamh, and stepped into the rushing water of the river, and was gone.

Avery looked at the Crow Girl. "I'm frightened," he said.

"As am I," she said. Then she smiled, big and bright and earnest. "But that's a good thing! Frightened means you've the sense to be afraid, and it's cowards who get things done, more often than not. Now. She's your friend, and part of your quest, like it or not. Which way would she go?"

Avery hesitated, thinking as hard as he could about Zib. He knew distressingly little about her, and maybe that was reasonable—it wasn't as if they'd ever met before, or like they'd had time to spare since their journey began. Everything had been place to place, and no pauses for care or comfort or the trading of stories. But maybe that was part of the answer. Zib liked to *move*. Of course she hadn't stayed still and waited for them to come and find her. He'd pushed her away, away from him. He'd left her vulnerable to the Page of Frozen Waters. She'd fallen, and then she'd gone somewhere.

Somewhere *else*.

If she had landed in the water—and he didn't want to think about her landing in the water, didn't want to think about her falling that far without anything to break her fall and hitting the surface of the river hard enough to break something else—she would have been swept along with it, away from the cliffs. If she had somehow managed to avoid the water, and avoid hurting herself too badly to move, she would probably have traveled in the same direction, because going back to the cliffs would have meant she wanted to find a way up to him, and she couldn't possibly want that, not after what he'd done.

"This way," he said, and pointed downriver, in the direction of the swirling, eddying rapids. "She would have gone this way."

The Crow Girl nodded. "So walk," she said, "and I'll follow." She burst into birds then, wings catching the sky as she swirled around him.

A crow landed on Avery's head. Another landed on each of his shoulders. Standing as straight and tall as he could, he began to walk.

After the bright colors and tangled vegetation of the protectorates held by the King of Coins and the Queen of Swords, the land claimed by the King of Cups was sere and strange. Bright stone glittered everywhere Avery looked, creating the impression of a world that had frozen solid, replacing everything that was soft and gentle with hard, rigid lines and sharp, cutting edges. The ground hurt his feet. The air hurt his throat. Even the crows seemed troubled by it; they circled back again and again, taking turns resting on his head and shoulders, letting him carry them along.

The more exhausted he became, the less he felt inclined to begrudge them. He envied them more than he would have thought possible, envied the fact that they had someone to carry them where they needed to go, while he needed to walk. He could remember, dimly, a time when he'd been small enough to be carried by his parents, their arms warm and safe around him, their strength extending to become his own. But that was in the past, in the safe, sensible world on the other side of the wall, and he was here, and it was his turn to be the strong one.

"I don't think I like to be the strong one," he muttered sourly to himself. "I don't think I like it at all."

The crow currently atop his head cawed in sympathy, and dug its claws a little deeper into his hair, holding tight as Avery walked on.

Avery couldn't have said how long he had been walking. It felt like it had been longer than a day, but that couldn't be true, because the light had never changed. The sun was hidden somewhere far away, behind the layers on layers of fog and mist and cloud, and everything was gray, gray, gray. It was not so bright as noon, nor so dark as midnight, but seemed to exist in an eternal gloomy middle space, unchanging, unchangeable. Still Avery walked on, until he wasn't sure he could go any farther.

He was tired. He thought he had never really known what tired was before today: he had *heard* of being tired, but he'd never really *felt* it. Tired went all the way down to his bones, wrapping around them like ribbons, until his legs were lead and his arms were sacks of sand suspended from his shoulders. Tired sapped the faint remaining color out of the world, turning everything dull and lifeless. Tired hung weights from his eyelashes. Whenever he blinked, he thought his eyes might refuse to open again.

There was a bundle of rags on the riverbank, covered in glittering silver dust, like fish scales or moonlight. Avery paused. Rags didn't normally have bare, dirty feet, or tangled, uncombed hair.

Avery found that he could run after all. The crows lifted off his head and shoulders, flying around him in a frantic, crowing cloud as he ran toward the bundle, toward the body, toward the girl he had walked so far to save. The crows settled on the nearby rocks, cawing and screaming, until everything was noise and nothing was the way it ought to be. He kept running until he had reached Zib's side. Then and only then he dropped to his knees, reaching for her, rolling her over.

"Zib," he said, breathless. "Zib, are you okay? Please be okay. I didn't mean any of the things I said before, really I didn't. I only need you to be all right. Please, please, for me, please be all right, please be okay, *please.*"

Her hair covered her face, obscuring it. The crows cried and cried as he pushed it aside, revealing not the wide, friendly features of the girl from the wall but the sharp, somehow predatory face of the Page of Frozen Waters, who smiled her razorblade smile as she pulled away from his hands and sat smoothly, seamlessly up. What he had taken for Zib's hair slid off her head, revealing itself for a mass of tangled water weeds.

"Lose something?" the Page asked. She glanced past him to the crows. Her smile faded. "You're a fool to show your faces here. We don't love traitors in this protectorate."

The crows took off, launching themselves skyward in a great flutter of black wings. The Page returned her attention to Avery, smile blooming once again.

"I never expected you to follow her this far," she said. "You're all alone now, little boy, but you intrigue me enough that I'll make you an offer. You should consider it closely, because you'll never hear its like again."

She stood, as easy as the sun shining through the clouds, and held her hands out toward him, like she expected him to take them willingly, to let her draw him easily in.

"Come with me," she said. "I can see that you're a child who likes ease and order, who likes to know how things will fall together. In the court of my king, fire always burns, water is always wet. Things do as they're told. We can give you everything you want, everything you need. I can make you a prince, if you'll let me, and perhaps one day, all this will be yours."

Avery blinked at her slowly. There was something wrong with her offer, something wicked and cruel, but it was hard for him to see it. He was *so* tired, and of course she hadn't been Zib, because why would Zib make things easy on him like that? Zib didn't make things easy on anyone, not even herself. Maybe he *should* listen to the Page of Frozen Waters. Maybe he should go with her to meet the King of Cups—Zib had met the Queen of Swords, after all, and it seemed only fair that each of them should have the opportunity to spend time with royalty. He'd never seen a real king before. The King of Cups must be awfully important, to have control over a place like this, to have someone like the Page of Frozen Waters at his command. Why, he might just be the most important, most magical person in the whole world! How could going and paying proper respects hurt anything?

Avery reached his hand out toward the Page of Frozen Waters, who reached back. Their fingers were only inches apart when three things happened, very, very quickly and at the same time:

A crow landed on Avery's shoulder and pecked him briskly in the side of the head, not quite breaking the skin, but setting his ears ringing like church bells, and

A sword came flying out of the river, the blade ripe with rust and blossoming with frost, the hilt studded with tiny crystals, rounded and sanded down by the motion of the water, until they became safe to hold, and

The Page of Frozen Waters suddenly looked less like a pleasantly smiling girl a few years older than Avery was, and more like a waterlogged corpse that had somehow forgotten that it was no longer meant to be up and moving around. Her skin had a soft, spongy-looking quality to it, and her hair was tangled with waterweeds, not the natural, exuberant tangle of Zib's hair, which had never met a hairbrush it didn't want to steal, or the feathery chaos of the Crow Girl's hair, or even the gentle disarray of Niamh's hair. This was an elf knot, the sort of snarl that could be corrected only with prayer and a pair of scissors, and no one who would allow their hair to become so uncontrolled and uncontrollable could possibly understand what it was to be a child who believed in starched shirts and polished shoes and keeping his word because it was right, and not because he wanted to.

Avery recoiled, one hand dipping to grab the sword in automatic defensiveness. He raised its blunted edge toward the Page of Frozen Waters, and the rust and ice fell away from the blade in a shivering sheet, leaving behind what looked like a sharpened razor made of glass, so sharp that it could slice the very air in two. It was impossible. He no longer knew quite what that word was meant to mean.

The Page of Frozen Waters recoiled. The crow on Avery's shoulder cawed furious victory. The Page narrowed her eyes.

"If that's what you choose, that's what you've chosen," she said. "Don't think this will be forgotten, either of you." She pointed a finger at the crow, the gesture sharp and furious, before making a shooing gesture with the whole of her hand.

The crow fell.

Avery whirled around, surprise overtaking anger, then transforming into horror. "No!" he yelped, the sword falling from his fingers as he dropped to his knees and gathered the fallen crow in his hands. The tiny, feathered body was stiff, its eyes open and already glazing over.

He barely heard the soft splash from behind him. When he turned, the Page of Frozen Waters was gone.

"That's not fair," he said. Niamh, who he assumed had thrown him the sword, did not appear or reply. "It's not *fair,*" he said again, louder. "She didn't do anything to you!"

"Oh, but I did, didn't I?" said the Crow Girl, sounding wearier than he had ever heard her sound before. He turned, and there she was, in her black dress and her bare feet, standing a few feet away. None of her seemed to be missing, but it was impossible to see every part of a person, wasn't it? People were like treasure chests, full of secrets that never saw the light of day. That crow could have been almost any part of her, and its loss might kill her slowly, or it might not kill her at all, but either way, it was gone. It had saved him, and it had died for its trouble.

Gingerly, she reached down and took the crow from his hands, cradling it against her chest. She looked at it with a depth of sorrow Avery wouldn't have believed possible. He remembered his own mother looking at him like that, when he'd skinned his knees or come home from school crying over some playground fight or other. The Crow Girl sighed.

"Gone," she said. "This was a part of me and now it's gone, and it's never going to come back again, and I don't know what it was before it left me; I can't know, because once a thing is broken past repairing, it doesn't return. I should be angry, I suppose—she did this to punish me more than to punish you—and I should be afraid, since she could do this to any other part of me she likes, but all I am is sad. Is that strange, that I should be more sad over this than over anything else?"

"I don't think so," whispered Avery. He bent and picked up the sword that had been flung from the river. Niamh was still nowhere to be seen. He didn't even know for sure that the blade had come from her. He simply assumed, because he knew no one else who could have done it. Quartz had no reason to be here, and the owls . . . owls did not, for the most part, swim.

"I'm glad," said the Crow Girl. Gently, she pushed the dead crow into the black feathers at her breast. It slipped inside with ease, and when she pulled her hands away, it didn't fall. Tears ran down her cheeks, slow and heavy and oil-slick bright. She looked at Avery and smiled, unevenly. "I suppose my side is set now; I suppose there's no going back. She shouldn't have done that. She shouldn't have done any of this. Let's break her like a bone and leave her for the sun to steal."

Avery, who didn't trust himself to speak, simply nodded. Zib needed them.

TEN
WHAT ISN'T YOURS

"I've been here before," said the Crow Girl, and started walking toward the gray and unforgiving cliff. "I was here for longer than anyone should have been, and the King knows my name, even though I gave it up and can't know it anymore, and when I left, I said I'd never come back again. I still know the way, though. I can still take us where we need to be."

"How do you know where we need to be?"

"We've seen the Page and paid a price, and stories take a certain shape here, if you let them. We're in it now. There's no going back to where we were."

Avery clutched his sword. He would rather have had his ruler, but that was lost now, along with the shine from his shoes, and so very many other things. "Is it safe?"

"Is anything safe? Walk outside on a clear spring morning and you can still find yourself beaten and broken on the dewy ground. There's no such thing as 'safe,' and anyone who tells you there is is lying, either to themselves, or to you. Or to both, I suppose. Some people are surprisingly good at lying to themselves." The Crow Girl stopped at the base of the cliff, looking up. "Even I'm surprisingly good at lying to myself. I said I'd never come back, but here I am, and I suppose I knew I would be as soon as I pulled you out of the mud. Lies always come back to bite you in the end."

"So it's dangerous," said Avery.

"Very," said the Crow Girl, and began to climb.

Avery hesitated, looking from the Crow Girl to the cliff to the sword in his hand. Zib was up there somewhere. Zib needed him. No one had ever needed him before, not really, not like that. He didn't owe it to her to try, exactly, but he felt he should. He felt like, given time, he should owe her the world.

The Crow Girl climbed. Avery followed.

There were narrow stairs cut into the side of the mountain, all but invisible from any distance away; by watching where the Crow Girl put her feet, he found that he could keep himself anchored to the cliffside, and thus keep himself from falling. He didn't look back, and he didn't look down. He had heard, somewhere, that looking back—that looking down—was the most dangerous thing a person could do while they were climbing up a mountain. He had no reason to think the adults who had told him this were lying.

As for the Crow Girl, she seemed to find every crack and fissure in the rock, driving her fingers into them and holding on fast. The feathers that made up her dress and tangled in her hair fluttered in the wind that blew around them, making her seem alien and impossibly strange. She didn't look back either. Avery thought that looking back must be *very* frightening, if the girl who knew how to fly wasn't willing to do it either. He wanted to drop the sword and free his other hand to help him climb, but didn't dare; he might need it, and soon.

He spared a thought for Niamh, who must still be in the river, who had probably given him the sword. She didn't know what was going on; she might never know. Like Quartz, like the owls, she had been left behind. The Up-and-Under seemed to do that quite a lot. It offered him companions, and then, one way or another, it whisked them away.

"I won't let them take you away," he muttered, and he didn't know whether he was talking to Zib or to the Crow Girl, and the both of them kept on climbing, kept on climbing, kept on climbing toward the sky.

The Crow Girl hesitated only once, when her questing fingers found the top of the cliff: he saw her reach up, catch hold of nothing, and pull her hands back down. She tucked her chin down against her chest, and when she began to speak, although her voice was low, he could hear every word.

"What happens next . . . I'm free, I'm my own bird and my own girl and the Queen of Swords is the only one who holds me at all, but the King of Cups made me. I was his once, and he might forget that he doesn't own me anymore. If he tries to take me, I may have to run away to keep him from doing it. I would be . . . I would be more dangerous to you in his keeping than I would be able to help. Do you understand?" Her tone was pained. She was begging him, she was pleading with him not to be angry.

Avery realized her words hurt in two directions at the same time. Thinking she might leave him hurt. Thinking she might be in danger if she didn't hurt even more. "Sure I do," he said. "I know you'll find us again. You're like the improbable road. You always come back."

The Crow Girl was quiet for a time before she said, "That's the nicest thing anyone has ever said to me," and untucked her chin, and raised her hand, and pulled herself over the edge of the cliff, onto whatever solid ground lay beyond.

Avery didn't want to follow her. He wanted to run, to go back to the bottom where Niamh was waiting and the Page of Frozen Waters wasn't. Instead, he reached up with his free hand, and pulled himself up after her, onto a sheet of ground rimed with bone-white frost. The air was so cold that it burned his skin, hurting him.

There was a long stretch of open, icy ground. On it was a throne, and on it sat a very old man, his skin crusted over with sheets of ice, his hair and beard and eyebrows tangled with still more, making him look ancient and aged and weary. Three girls who looked like the Crow Girl in all the ways that didn't matter, and nothing like her in any of the ways that did, knelt at his feet. They didn't shiver. The feathers atop their heads were sleek and shining, as if they didn't feel the cold, while the feathers atop the head of *his* Crow Girl, *their* Crow Girl, stood at shuddering attention.

There was a cage, and in it was Zib, shivering hard enough to make up for the Crow Girls who weren't, her hands wrapped tight around the bars, like she thought she could pull them out of their sockets and set herself free. There was a feather in her hair, red as fresh-spilled blood, banded with darker streaks, and it hadn't come from a crow, and Avery couldn't have said where she had found it, but he knew it hadn't been there when she'd fallen. In front of the cage stood the Page of Frozen Waters, a trident of ice held loosely in her hands and a slight smirk on her face as she gazed at the pair of them.

"So," she said. "You decided not to be cowards after all. How nice. I've been meaning to finish things with her"—a nod toward the Crow Girl—"since she decided to run away. It's always sad when someone refuses the good things you offer them, isn't it?"

The King of Cups, frozen in his throne, said nothing, only blinked lazily and watched them with the disinterested air of a man who had seen little of interest in a very, very long time.

Avery took a step forward. His knees were shaking. His teeth were chattering. His whole skeleton felt like it was coming apart at the joints, like it was going to fall into so many bones on the floor. He wanted to turn. He wanted to run away. He didn't belong here. This was between the Crow Girl and the man she'd run away from, between Zib and the Page of Frozen Waters. This wasn't his fight at all.

But Zib was clinging to the bars of her cage, and he could see the black feathers pushing against her skin, trying to burst free, to turn her into a Crow Girl like all the others. She wouldn't be Zib if he let that happen. She wouldn't be Hepzibah, either. She'd be something else, something wilder and stranger and not his at all. He hadn't known her long enough to care as much as he did. He cared anyway. He couldn't let the Page have her.

"You have to give her back," he said. "She's my friend, and she doesn't belong to you."

The Page of Frozen Waters smiled her razorblade smile. "Why should I?" she asked.

"Because . . ." Avery took a deep breath. "Because I asked, and because I'll cut you into ribbons if you don't."

The King of Cups blinked, a slow and thoughtful gesture, like a stone rolling in the depths of the sea. The Page of Frozen Waters narrowed her eyes.

"I think *not,*" she said. "I'm better than you, and I'm bigger than you, and I'm faster than you for all of that. If you try, I'll cut your heart out and give it to my lord and master as a token of my esteem."

"You'll have to go through me first," said the Crow Girl.

The Page of Frozen Waters snorted. "Through you?

The coward? I think *not*, broken little thing that you are. You don't even know how much of you has flown away. Leave, before you find yourself remembered."

The other Crow Girls watched with blank, avian eyes, neither approving nor disapproving, and Avery shivered again—this time, not with cold. There was something wrong with them, something *missing*.

The Page of Frozen Waters followed his gaze. Her smile widened.

"They thought they were allowed to fight, and fly, and flee," she said. "They came before *that* one"—she gestured sharply to the Crow Girl—"but they tried to follow after her, and that simply can't be allowed. Your heart won't be the first one I cut from its moorings, nor the first to freeze. It's peaceful. You'll see, if you keep threatening your betters, just how cold a heart can grow."

"Get out of here, Avery!" shouted Zib. There was a hint of a crow's harsh caw in her words as she shook the bars of her cage. "It doesn't matter if you can't go home without me, I'll be fine, I'll be . . ." Her voice broke, tapering out. Finally, she whispered, "I always wanted to fly."

"I'm not leaving without you," said Avery. He tried to keep an eye on the Page of Frozen Waters, his hands tight on the hilt of his sword. It was sharp. It was so sharp. He was sure it could cut through anything he needed it to cut. He was less sure about his own ability to cut through a living person. Even the Page of Frozen Waters was alive, and deserved to stay that way.

"Then you're not leaving, child," said the Page of

Frozen Waters. "I'm sure you'll come to love it here. I did." She raised her trident into place, as if to strike.

The Crow Girl stepped in front of Avery. "No," she said, voice clear and calm.

The Page of Frozen Waters faltered. "Move," she ordered.

"No," the Crow Girl repeated. Then she laughed. "It's so easy, isn't it? No, and no, and no. There's a glory in refusal that I never thought I'd see. No to you. No forever. I won't move, and you won't hurt the boy, and you won't have the girl. No."

"You feathered fool," said the Page. "You don't have the right to stop me anymore. You gave it up when you landed here."

"Did I?" asked the Crow Girl. "I don't remember, so I suppose it doesn't matter. If I can't remember saying that I wouldn't do a thing, I can't be expected to abide by it." She winked to Avery then, bold and broad, and he stiffened in sudden excitement, realizing what he had to do.

His mother *hated* crows. They stole crops from her garden and frightened the neighborhood dogs so that they started barking in the early hours of the morning, breaking the peace into shards that couldn't be pieced back together. But most of all, she hated the way they worked together. One crow would distract a cat while three more emptied out the food dish; one crow would swoop in front of a car while another hurried the fledglings away from the road. The Crow Girl was doing that for him. She was puffing her feathers and raising

her voice and keeping the Page of Frozen Waters looking at anything but him.

He'd seen crows dead in the road before, hit by
cars while they were trying to take care of their flocks,
and he'd seen crows with broken, buckshot-peppered
wings, shot by farmers who wanted to feed their cats
more than they wanted to feed the crows. What she was
doing was dangerous. He owed it to her to take the gift
she was offering, and to take it quickly.

Zib's eyes widened as he moved toward the cage. She
seemed to understand what he was doing, though;
she was silent as she let go of the bars and moved away.
He took the point of the sword and slipped it into the
lock, jiggling it until it went as deep as it could possibly
go. Then he began to twist.

Avery had never picked a lock before, and had never
done *anything* with a sword before, and he was pretty
sure he was doing this wrong. But as he twisted, the lock
grew stiff with frost, and finally, it splintered, breaking
with a soft cracking noise. He dropped the sword in his
surprise. It clattered against the frozen ground.

The Page of Frozen Waters whipped around, her
eyes going wide as she realized what had happened.
"You!" she shouted. "How *dare* you!" She raised her
trident, stabbing it toward Avery in a gesture clearly
intended to pierce his heart.

Avery thought of the crows in the road, and knew
that he was finished; knew that he couldn't move
quickly enough to get out of the way. He closed his
eyes.

The sound of ice shattering shocked him out of his stillness. He opened his eyes again, and there was Zib, standing between him and the Page of Frozen Waters, even as the Crow Girl had done—but unlike the Crow Girl, she was holding the sword, and had it raised in front of her, stopping the Page's trident from striking him. Two of the tines on the trident had shattered into so many frozen shards, and the third was locked against her blade, unable to separate.

The Page, eyes gone wide and almost frightened, was standing her ground, but Avery thought she wouldn't continue to do that for very long. She didn't seem like the sort of person who was very good at being afraid. "You can't fight me," she said. "You belong to me."

"I still have my slingshot, and I still have a dime and three acorns, and I guess as long as I have those, I don't belong to anyone, because property doesn't have property," snarled Zib. She twisted the sword, knocking the trident from the Page's hands, so that it fell to the ground. It shattered where it landed. She stepped forward. "I don't like people who put me in cages."

"Oh," said the Crow Girl. Her voice was very soft.

Avery turned.

The King of Cups was rising from his throne.

He moved slowly, sheets of ice cracking and falling away with every gesture. They carried the years with them; the man who finally, glacially came to his feet was no older than Avery's father, and had the same implacable dignity, as if no one would ever dare to question him in his place of power. This *was* his place of power, absolutely, his protectorate in a world that was otherwise set against him. The Page of Frozen Waters turned and fled to his side, sliding half behind him, letting him be her barrier.

The Crow Girl did not move. Did not even seem to breathe as the King of Cups stepped toward them, his eyes going from her feathered form to Avery, and finally to Zib.

"You," he said. "You were to be mine."

There was a question in his voice, a confusion, as if he couldn't understand why Zib would be anything other than captive and cloaked in feathers. But her skin was smooth, and there were no feathers in her hair. Strange she might be, and dirty and disheveled, but she was still wholly and completely human.

"I never said that," said Zib tightly. "I wasn't looking for you. I didn't ask for a cage."

The King turned, still slow, and looked at the Page. "Is this true?" he asked.

"She came here," protested the Page. "If they come here, they want your blessings! That's how it's always been, and how it's meant to be! She didn't have to say anything for me to know what she wanted."

The King frowned. "We can't keep what's been improperly taken," he said. "You know that."

"I didn't mean—"

"But you did it." He looked to the Crow Girl. "You, though . . . you belong to me."

"I belong to the Queen of Swords now," she said,

voice small. "You let me go, and she took me in. I'm not your bird and not your girl and not your pretty toy."

"And if I told you I'd let the children go, if only you'd agree to stay?"

The Crow Girl went still. Avery looked at her, and Zib looked at her, and both of them knew that she wasn't going to save them: that she would, in the end, only be able to save herself.

"I would say that you were wrong to do that to me," said the Crow Girl. "I would say that when you let me go, you never said anything about tricking me back one day. I would say a strong king doesn't need to play that kind of game with the people he claims to be protecting. I would say it wasn't fair. The children don't belong to you, and that means you shouldn't be using them for bargaining. But I would say that if that was the price, I'd do it. I'll never be yours. I'll never be still, or quiet, or good. But I would stay."

The King of Cups sighed heavily. Zib shivered, inching closer to Avery, as if he could protect her from the cold.

"Fine," he said. "All of you, get gone. I want nothing more to do with you."

"But—" began the Page of Frozen Waters.

He turned and looked at her, and she became very still, like a rat facing the narrow-eyed gaze of the family cat.

The Crow Girl grabbed Avery by one arm, and Zib by the other, and ran, as fast as she could, for the edge of the cliff. The children let her haul them in her wake, until she ran past the end of the stone, out into empty nothingness.

The fall was sharp, and short, and brutal. Zib screamed. Avery wailed. The Crow Girl burst into birds, all the pieces of the murder swirling around them in a skirl of dark feathers, wings beating frantically, until the children realized they were no longer falling but were rolling down a bridge of birds, their descent slowed to something stately, something almost *kind*.

When they reached the ground, the Crow Girl re-formed, dropping to her knees on the rocky shore and panting. Finally, she looked up through her feathered bangs and smiled wanly.

"See?" she said. "Got you out. I'm clever."

"Yes," said Avery. "You are." He looked to Zib, then. "But what *happened*?"

Zib took a deep breath, and said, "I met an owl . . ."

ELEVEN
WHERE ZIB WENT,
AND HOW IT HAPPENED

Oak soared on vast red wings, and Zib snuggled into the owl's feathers, warm and safe and lost. It was strange, to think that she could be safe and lost at the same time; the two conditions felt as if they ought to contradict one another, leaving her either safe at home or lost and in danger, but with the owl all around her, the world seemed like a kinder place.

The fog was more shades of gray than she had ever thought possible, pale as a pearl and dark as a stone after the rain. She watched it swirl around them until her eyelids felt heavy and her whole body felt thick, the way it sometimes did when she stayed up too far past her bedtime. She couldn't think of how long it had been since she'd slept.

Surely the school day was over by now. Surely her father was home from dropping off other people's children, stepping into the living room, hanging his coat on the peg, and calling, "Where's my little piece of pumpkin pie?" with the expectant air of a man whose questions were answered more often than not.

Her mother, wrapped in her painting as she so often was, probably wouldn't have noticed that she had never come home, had never grabbed an apple from the counter or called hello before rushing back off to the woods, back to her private adventures. She'd say that Zib had been there, surely Zib had been there, and so neither of them would worry. Not until the sun was going down and she was still nowhere to be seen.

How long would it be before they moved from confusion to anger, and then finally to fear? Would they call their friends—surely they must have friends, friends couldn't be a thing that ended with childhood, no one would ever choose to grow up if they couldn't be adults and have friends at the same time—and go into the woods looking for her?

Would they find the wall?

Zib didn't think they would.

She was so sunk in the owl's warmth and in her own uneasy thoughts that she didn't notice the air getting colder around them, or the fog getting darker, until it was less pearl and more stone, until she could barely see through her almost-closed eyes.

Then Oak cried out, a high, pained sound, and fell

out of the sky, twisting around and around like a leaf caught in a sudden gale. The great owl slammed into the ground, Zib cushioned by the feathers of its breast, and she gasped, the wind knocked out of her by the impact.

"You shouldn't be here, bird." The voice was old, and cold, and almost disdainful. Zib opened her eyes and beheld the man who stood above her.

He was tall, and thin, and looked even older than he sounded, as old as wishes, as old as winter. His hair was white and his eyes were blue, and ice formed and cracked on his eyelashes, falling away every time he blinked. His robes were heavy velvet patterned with cascades of water flowing from weighty chalices, and she knew him for the King of Cups, and she knew she was in danger, for all that his attention was wholly focused on the owl.

"I was helping the girl," said Oak, one wing curling protectively around her.

The King of Cups tilted his head before turning his attention on Zib. "Were you, now?" he asked. "Hello, child. You must be precious indeed, if old Oak would risk capture for your sake. What is your name?"

"Hepzibah Jones," she replied, before she could stop herself. She didn't want to give the King of Cups her proper name—had not, in fact, intended it—but something about the way he spoke left no room for argument, no room for hesitation.

"You are not of my protectorate, are you?"

"No." She hesitated. "Sir."

The King of Cups laughed. "A polite child is a rare treasure! Tell me, child, do you *wish* to be of my protectorate? To be kept, and comforted, and safe, for all the days of your life? You could be happy here."

Zib thought he must be lying. Adults didn't smile that fixed, glossy smile, or speak with so much sharpness, when they were telling her the truth. Oak was shivering behind her, with fear as much as cold, and she felt a stab of pity. The owl had only been trying to help her. This fight—if it was a fight—was hers, and hers alone.

"No, thank you," she said, and moved so that she was no longer in the sheltering coil of Oak's wing but was standing between the great owl and the king. "I am on the improbable road to the Impossible City, you see, and I haven't the time to stop and be a part of someone else's protectorate. I need to find my friends."

"They must not be terribly good friends, to be lost so easily."

Zib bristled. "They weren't *lost*. I was taken away from them. A dreadful girl who calls herself the Page of Frozen Waters pushed me off the side of a cliff, and I fell for quite a long way, and Oak came to stop me from being harmed. Now I'm on my way back to where I should have been, so I can finish going where I'm supposed to be. Please, do you know the way?"

The King of Cups smiled like a winter storm rolling in. He looked younger when he smiled. He looked no less terrible. "The Page of Frozen Waters is a part of my protectorate," he said. "She gathers the lost things and brings them to me, and it seems she has gathered you, because here you are, and aren't you lovely? Aren't you rare and fine? I'll make you better, child. I'll make you more than you ever thought you'd be. You'll be happy in my company, for you'll know that you're precisely where you belong."

"Run," whispered Oak. There was no flurry of wings, for owls are silent in flight, but there was a sudden feeling of absence, and Zib knew that the great owl was gone.

Zib couldn't blame her brief companion for fleeing. She would have fled, had she known how, although she thought she wouldn't have been quite so quick to leave someone else behind—she thought she would have stayed until she knew Oak could be free, if she had been the one with wings. Still, she took the owl's parting advice seriously, stepping nervously backward as she prepared to run.

Something sharp pressed against the skin between her shoulders, stopping her. She could no more keep moving, knowing it would impale her, than she could have flown away.

"I see you found your way," said the Page of Frozen Waters, sweet and bright and overjoyed, and Zib knew that she was lost.

"She's lovely," said the King of Cups. "Wherever did you find her?"

"The Queen of Swords gave her and her companions a skeleton lock," said the Page. "They were meant to land nearer to the Impossible City, but it was a cold wind that blew them, and I was able to convince it to freeze and bring them here instead."

"Companions?" asked the King.

"A boy child and the traitor Crow. They're somewhere off in the mist. It's no matter. I knew this was the one you'd want."

Zib balled her fists and stomped her foot and said, "I'm right *here*! It's rude to talk about a person like they aren't in the room when they *are*!"

"Ah, but this isn't a room, and moreover, I am a king; the rules are different for me." The King of Cups stepped smoothly forward and grasped Zib's chin in his cold, cold hand. With the blade at her back, she couldn't even pull away. "Yes, you'll do nicely, child. You'll learn to love it here, with me, and I'll give you something all children want, in their secret hearts, which are hungry, hungry things, and will devour whatever they are offered. I'll give you *wings*."

Zib tried to shake her head, to break his hold on her, but her body refused to listen, and the cold swept over her, and it was easier to be still; it was easier to be calm, and quiet, and frozen, and cold, cold, cold, and then she was falling again, falling into the mist, which had no end and no beginning, which was everything . . .

As she fell, she thought she felt feathers brush against her cheek.

I am sorry, whispered a voice. Meadowsweet: the first of the three great owls. How queer, to hear that long-left bird speaking to her here. *I am not strong enough.*

Strong enough for what? Zib thought, but could not speak, and then the voice was gone, and she was alone, again, and falling.

I am sorry, whispered another voice. Broom: second and coldest of the great owls. He sounded genuinely unhappy, which did not make things any better. *I am not swift enough.*

Swift enough for what? Zib thought, and did not expect an answer.

I am sorry, whispered a third voice. Oak, and this voice ached most of all, for of the three great owls, Oak was the only one to have left her. *I am not sure enough.*

Sure enough for what? Zib thought, and hit the ground with what felt like force enough to break every bone in her body. Her eyes, which she had not been aware of closing, snapped open.

She was in a cage.

The bars were black iron, rimed with ice and studded with decorative swirls that were probably lovely to the people *outside* the cage, but created a field of spikes and sharp edges for the person *inside* the cage. Zib scrambled to her feet, looking wildly around. The cage was on a stretch of wide, flat, frozen ground. Nearby, there was a throne. On the throne sat the King of Cups, and around him . . .

She froze for a moment, trying to make sense of what she saw. Her eyes, adjusting to the scene, began to find the tiny differences in the three girls who sat arrayed around him, like faithful hounds surrounding their master. All of them were lithe and pale and dressed in gowns of black feathers, with more black feathers in their hair. If one had eyes that were a trifle larger than the other two, and one had a chin that was a trifle sharper, and one looked as if she might, upon standing, be a trifle taller, it didn't make much difference, for they were crow girls all, like copies of her Crow Girl, who was—she hoped, she wished, she prayed—still with Avery, and safe from the hand of this grasping king.

The Page of Frozen Waters popped up in front of her like a Jack from his box, a smile on her face and a needle in one hand. There was a black feather in her other hand, held tightly between her thumb and forefinger.

"Give me your arm," she said.

Zib, who was more sensible than Avery gave her credit for being, shrank back against the bars. "No."

"Give me your arm, or I will take it, and little as you think you'll like what's coming, you'll like that even less."

Reluctantly, Zib extended her arm, until the Page could lean into the cage, just enough to prick her with the needle. It was very sharp. A bead of blood welled immediately to the surface of the skin, and the Page wiped it away with the black feather, leaving no visible wound at all.

"There," she said, sounding quite satisfied. "That wasn't so difficult, was it? Everything is easier when you cooperate." Then she was gone, bounding away to whatever odd errands occupied a girl like her, in a place like this.

Zib huddled against the bars and shivered. It felt like things were shifting beneath her skin, like pieces of her that were meant to be perfectly still were finding the power to move around. She thought of the Crow Girl bursting into birds. She thought of her blood on the black feather, and she blinked back hot tears, and she wondered whether it would hurt when she came apart, when she stopped being *one* and started being *many.*

The King of Cups closed his eyes. Ice settled over him like a shroud. Zib held her breath, counting the seconds until she was sure he was asleep. Then she pulled the slingshot from her pocket, and one of the acorns she had been carrying for all this time, and pulled back the strap, taking careful aim at the crow girl with the sharpest chin. She had been told, more than once, that a chin that was too sharp was a thing boys would find unattractive when she got older, and she had seen nothing to indicate that she had been lied to. It stood to reason, then, that the King of Cups might find the sharpest chin the least attractive, and might spend the smallest amount of his attention on that particular crow girl.

Girls who are ignored can learn to be impossible, can learn to listen, and look, and learn more than they were ever meant to know. If she was going to find an ally here, she would find it in the crow girl with the least to lose.

She released the strap of her slingshot, and the acorn flew straight and true, hitting the crow girl in the shoulder, where there were no feathers to muffle the impact. The crow girl flinched but didn't make a sound, simply turned to regard Zib with curious avian eyes, the feathers in her hair standing very slightly on end. Zib made a come-closer gesture, beckoning her. The crow girl cocked her head to the side, considering. Then she looked to the King of Cups, as if measuring the depth of his slumber. Finally, she rose, and padded toward the cage where Zib was waiting.

Her feet were bare, her toes like talons. *All* their feet were bare, and unlike Zib, they didn't seem to feel the cold.

"Hello," she said, once she was close enough. Her voice was low, but she made no effort to whisper. "Are you going to join our flock? There were four of us once before, until the first one left. It would be nice to be four again. Four is a good number. Can't have a boy without four. But you're not a boy, are you? You move like a girl to me."

"Don't you mean I look like a girl?" asked Zib, curiosity briefly winning over panic.

"No. Why would I mean that? That's silly. No one looks like a girl, or a boy, or an elm tree, or anything else. Someone either *is* or *isn't* a thing, and the world can put as many layers on top of the thing as it likes; won't change what's underneath." The crow girl shrugged. "People say I look like a girl, but that won't ever make me one."

Zib blinked. "You're not? But I thought—"

"Oh, I'm a *crow* girl, but I'm not a *girl* girl." The crow girl's smile was swift, there and gone in an instant.

"I'm a murder. The skin's only for the outside people. The real me is all feathers and thorns, and not a girl at all. Are you going to be a part of our flock?"

"I don't want to be," whispered Zib.

"Oh," said the crow girl, face falling. "That doesn't mean you won't be."

"Please." Zib grabbed the bars of the cage, ignoring the way they bit into her palms. "Can you let me out of here? Is there a key you can bring me?"

"There's no key," said the crow girl. "The door opens when the Page wants it to open, and it closes when the Page wants it to close. It's like us, you see. It belongs to her. The King makes everything possible, and most of the time all he wants is for us to sit at his feet and smile and tell him how very clever he is, but the Page holds our jesses, and we don't fly without her permission. There's no key that can be stolen, no lock that can be picked. You'll be where you'll be until she says otherwise. But it's all right! It's all right. Once your heart shatters, you won't even feel the cold."

Zib wasn't sure what a heart was for, exactly: knew that grownups put a great deal of weight on whether or not she was listening to her heart over her head, knew that they were quite fond of telling her not to give it carelessly away. Even so, she couldn't imagine a heart was meant to shatter, or that it was an event which should be treated quite so lightly.

"Why will my heart shatter?" asked Zib.

"So that you can be a murder," said the crow girl, matter-of-factly. "I have so many hearts now, or I did, before the King of Cups decided that I didn't need them anymore. He must have been right, because I fly so much better now, and everything is fine, and I never feel the cold, not even as much as I did before he split me open and took away what wasn't wanted."

Zib swallowed. "I don't think I want that," she said. "Please, isn't there anything you can do to help me? I like being a girl. I like having only one heart, that hasn't been shattered or stolen. I want to stay the way I am, and not change into something else."

"I'm sorry," said the crow girl.

"Please."

The crow girl stood in silent thought for a long moment before turning and walking away, past the throne where the King of Cups slept and the other members of the flock sat silent attendance, until she was almost out of view. Then she knelt, picking something up from the frozen ground, and walked back.

It was a feather. A long red feather, banded with darker streaks, like a strip of paint peeled from the side of a barn. Zib recognized it at once, and when the crow girl slid it between the bars of the cage, she snatched it greedily, bringing it to her nose and breathing deeply in. It smelled, ever so faintly, of the great owl who had carried her here, who had tried to protect her, who had failed and fled.

"Oak," she breathed.

"Owls are good," said the crow girl. "Owls remember things. Crow girls don't. We're a poem in the process of being unwritten, a thought about to be unformed.

We forget because remembering is bad for us. If you can hold on to the feather, maybe you can remember. Maybe what's bad for us can be good for you, since you'd rather be a girl than a murder."

"Thank you," whispered Zib. She reached up and pulled one lock of hair free from the mass, separating it with quick, clever fingers before winding it around the shaft of the feather. When she let go, the feather hung so it almost brushed her cheek, held securely in place by her plaiting.

"It's all I can do," said the crow girl. Then she smiled. "You'll be happier when you're one of us. The King of Cups will make all manner of promises, because that's what he does, and then he'll break them all, because that's also what he does: a king may be a liar and not suffer for it one bit. But he'll tell you you'll be happier, and he'll mean it, because a shattered heart can never be broken, and a murder who looks like a girl who has no heart to break is the happiest thing in the world. You'll see. I promise, given time, you'll see."

The crow girl turned and walked back to the throne, settling into position alongside the rest of her flock. Zib fingered the acorns in her pocket and thought about trying again. It didn't seem like the best idea. If one crow girl couldn't help her, neither could the next, and she only had so many acorns; when they were gone, they were gone. What they could do against a king, she didn't know.

Settling to the floor of the cage, she pressed her back

as close to the bars as she could, and closed her eyes. She felt small, and cold, and afraid. If she slept for a time, maybe those things would be better. Or maybe she would have a dream that would tell her what to do, and when she woke, she would find her freedom like an apple, ready to be plucked.

Instead, when she opened her eyes, it was because she itched all over, as if she had rolled in a field of stinging nettles. She scratched at her arm, carefully at first, then with more and more vigor, trying to chase the itching away. It didn't work. The itching got worse, and worse, until she thought she might scratch her own skin off, trying to have done with it.

Her fingers found a tuft of what felt like stiffened, mud-matted hair at the bend of her elbow. She grabbed it and ripped it free, and the itching stopped, as suddenly as the air escaping from a popped soap bubble. She started to throw the offending bit of hair aside and froze, staring at it, unable to breathe.

It was a feather. A small black feather, like the kind of feather she might have expected to find on a baby crow, not yet long enough or stiff enough for flight, but more than long enough, more than stiff enough, to have no business at all growing out of her body. She looked at her arm. A small bead of blood stood up where the feather had been, bright red against her skin.

Silently, Zib began to cry.

She didn't know how long she'd been crying when the Page of Frozen Waters reappeared, popping up beside the cage with a bright smile on her face. "Hello again, new girl. How do you like your feathers? They don't fit so well beneath the skin, do they?"

"I hate you," said Zib, voice gone dull. "You are a terrible person."

"Maybe, but I'm not the one in the cage." The Page twinkled at her, as bright and cold and deadly as a star. "I'm not the one who'll be dressed in feathers and forgotten. You should be nicer to me while you have the choice. You won't, soon, and I'll remember what you said while you still thought you could be free."

Zib got up onto her knees, clutching the bars to bring herself as close as possible to the Page as she glared. "You are bad," she said. "You are rotten and twisted and awful inside, and you can dress me in feathers and make me a murder, but I know something you don't know."

The Page lost her smile, expression turning wary. "What's that?"

"The ground beneath your feet doesn't *glitter*," said Zib. "The improbable road has never chosen you, not even once, because if it had, you wouldn't be here; you'd be off on an adventure, not sitting by a man who lets you hurt people and doesn't tell you that it's wrong. You'd go to the Impossible City. You haven't because you can't. I could, if you opened this cage, and you can never take that away from me. I'll always be the girl who could do what you couldn't."

The Page of Frozen Waters hissed fury and reached into the air like she was reaching into a pocket, pulling out a trident that looked like it was made of nothing but ice. She pointed it at Zib. "I don't want your stupid city, and I don't want your useless road, and you're going to be mine to command, and there's *nothing you can do about it.*"

The owl feather in Zib's hair twisted, like it was trying to cup her hair; she heard voices, soft and distant but crystal clear, and she smiled.

"Oh," she said. "I think that's where you're wrong."

TWELVE

THE TRUTH ABOUT OWLS

"...and that's when you came," said Zib matter-of-factly. "You showed up just in time."

Zib stopped speaking. Avery stared at her for a moment, eyes wide and round and horrified, before he threw himself at her, wrapping his arms around her shoulders and pulling her as close as he could, holding her as tightly as a strand of ivy holds a tree.

"*Never* do that again," he commanded. "Never, *ever* do that again." Her skin was smooth under his hands, with no hint of quill or feather, but he knew he would see her bursting into birds in his nightmares for the rest of his life. He could be old, older than his parents, older than the trees, and still he'd see her coming apart, dissolving and flying away.

The Crow Girl was less dramatic, although no less concerned. "Let me see your arm," she commanded.

Silently, Zib obliged. The Crow Girl gripped her wrist, fingers surprisingly gentle despite their claw-like nails, and turned Zib's arm gingerly over as she studied the place where the feather had sprouted. Finally, she exhaled.

"They're going back to bone," she said. "All children have feathers on their bones, waiting for the chance to sprout and fly away. Sometimes the trick is in keeping them there."

"Children don't have *feathers*," said Avery, letting go of Zib so he could frown at the Crow Girl. "I would know."

"Maybe they don't where you come from, but here, in the Up-and-Under, they do, and you're here now, so what's true for one is true for all." The Crow Girl glanced at the ground. "The road's not here. We should find it and be on our way."

"Can we find Niamh, too?" asked Zib. "She shouldn't be alone."

"We can watch for her," said the Crow Girl. "Now come, come, come. We're still in *his* protectorate, and even if he let us go, he forgets things sometimes. He could forget forgiving us, and then we'd have to do this all again. But no one else forgets. That's the trouble with having a memory of ice. It melts, and you get the good again for the very first time, while the people all around you sharpen their swords against the bad."

"Swords . . ." said Avery. He glanced at the blade in Zib's hand, her fingers curled possessively around the hilt. "You should keep the sword. I don't think it was ever really meant for me. I don't want to fight people."

"I don't want to fight people either," said Zib, making no move to offer the sword back to him. "That doesn't mean I won't, if they make me. I'll keep you safe."

Avery smiled. "I know you will," he said.

The ground beneath their feet began to glitter, as if a fountain of fireflies had opened somewhere beneath the icy stone. Zib gasped in delight.

"The improbable road!" she said. "It's found us!"

"It always does," said the Crow Girl smugly. "Come. Come. We have a long way left to go."

She began to walk, and the children followed her. Avery reached out, almost timidly, and slid the fingers of his free hand into Zib's. She glanced at him and smiled, sidelong and shy, and everything was going to be all right. They had survived the court of the King of Cups; the feathers under Zib's skin were gone. Niamh would find them, rising out of the river alongside the road like a fountain, and they would reach the Impossible City, and they would go *home*.

Home. It was a shining star of an idea, impossible and infinitely appealing. It was a dream that had no ending and no beginning, only a complex, clean middle. Nothing would have changed. Oh, his parents might be angry at him for missing a day of school, but his mother would cover his face in kisses, and his father would clap a hand on his shoulder, welcoming him back to a world where children didn't have feathers wrapped around their bones, where fruit always tasted the same way, and where girls never burst into crows.

Girls. He looked at Zib. She was smiling as she walked, the sword in her hand looking like it had always belonged there, like she had been somehow incomplete before she held a weapon against the world. She was scrawny and scruffy and her hair was somehow more tangled than it had been before, standing up and out from her head like a thorn briar, equally full of secrets. She was not the kind of child his parents had always encouraged him to play with, the kind who would grow up to be serious and quiet and just like him. She was loud, and wild, and his mother would frown at the state of her hands, and his father would frown at the state of her clothes, and it would be so much easier to believe this journey hadn't changed him if he was only willing to leave her behind.

He wasn't willing to leave her behind.

The realization blossomed like a flower in his chest, and he tightened his hand on hers, until his grip was hard enough that she glanced at him again, questioning and confused. The Crow Girl walked in front of them, blissfully oblivious.

"What's wrong?" asked Zib.

Avery hesitated before blurting, "I don't understand why there are so many owls. I've never seen this many owls in my whole *life*, and now they're everywhere. Why are there so many owls?"

"I don't know," said Zib. "I like them, though." She didn't have a hand free to touch the feather in her hair, and so she tossed her head a little, so that it brushed her cheek like a caress. "They've all been nice."

"They must want something," said Avery staunchly. He felt confident of that, at least: his parents had always told him that people were only nice when they wanted something, and that the appropriate thing to do was smile, and nod, and walk away as soon as he possibly could. "I don't know what owls want."

"The same thing everyone wants," said the Crow Girl, without turning. "A warm place to sleep, a soft place to land, and something to fill their bellies when the wind blows cold. No one's as different from anyone else as they want to think they are. No one's as the same, either. It's the paradox of living."

"What's a paradox?" asked Zib.

"Two places to tie your boat," said the Crow Girl, and cawed harsh, impolite laughter to the sky.

Avery frowned, and was on the verge of saying something when strong talons gripped his shoulders and yanked him off the improbable road, up into the cloudy air. It was so abrupt that his hand left Zib's, so that she was holding nothing but the memory of where he had been, and that his shineless shoes came quite off of his feet, remaining behind on the improbable road as he vanished into the fog.

Zib whirled around, sword raised, but there was nothing for her to cut. The Crow Girl squawked and spun, her feathers fluffed out in all directions, but there was nothing for her to startle.

"Where . . . where did he go?" asked Zib.

"I don't know," said the Crow Girl.

"Get him back! You have to get him back!"

"I don't know how."

Zib stared at Avery's shoes and then up into the fog. It was difficult to remember exactly where Avery had been before he went away. He had taken his shadow with him, which seemed suddenly, unspeakably rude, even though Zib had never thought of it that way before. Shadows should stay behind when someone was planning on coming back, to mark the place they were *going* to be.

A hand touched her shoulder. She looked up to find the Crow Girl smiling at her encouragingly, the shadow of a strain in her avian eyes.

"It's all right," she said. "He'll be back, safe and sound, you'll see."

"How do you know?" asked Zib.

"Why, because we're on the improbable road to the Impossible City, and right now, what could be more improbable, or impossible, than your friend coming back to you?" The Crow Girl smiled a bright and earnest smile. "There's no possible way it could happen, and that means it's virtually guaranteed."

Zib stared at her for a moment before bursting, noisily, into tears. She was still crying when the great blue owl swept down from the sky and grabbed her by the shoulders, yanking her off her feet and carrying her away.

The Crow Girl stood where she was, gaping at the absence of both her traveling companions. She tilted her head back and looked at the sky, which was absent of both children and great owls. She began to frown.

"That wasn't very kind," she said. "They were mine to look after, and you took them." She knew, somewhere in the jumbled back of her mind—which was something like a rummage sale, all broken pottery and old shoes with holes in the bottoms and treasures whose owners have forgotten why they were so precious in the first place—that she needed those children. They were taking her somewhere, somewhere she needed to be, somewhere she couldn't go on her own. They *mattered*, and now she had lost them.

She needed to get them back. That much was terribly clear. She could break into birds and take to the sky, but thinking when she was more than one thing was *hard*. It made her heads hurt and her wings forget which way they were supposed to be flapping. Once, she'd tried to fly up and read over someone's shoulder, and she'd found herself flying backward for the better part of a day. It hadn't been pleasant, that was for sure and certain, and she didn't want to do it again. She could save someone who was falling, but she couldn't braid their hair.

More, and more dangerously, the King of Cups was so awfully near, and crows were so much simpler. They didn't think about things like freedom and cruelty. They thought about food and safety and knowing that there were no predators to take their neighbors or their suppers away. She'd had all those things with the King. It was only the ability to choose her own direction that she'd been missing.

She was still thinking about what she was going to do next when a pair of talons clamped down on her shoulders and she was lifted off the ground. Her whole body shivered, her skin aching to open like a wound and let her fly in a dozen directions at the same time, away from whatever had seized hold of her. She swallowed the feeling down and tilted her head back, looking up at the pale pink belly of the great red owl.

Oak returned her gaze, implacable as ever. "I am sorry for this interruption," said the owl. "Your friends are waiting."

The owl's voice was steady and cold, and it made the Crow Girl's heart hurt inside her chest, unable to decide how it should feel. She managed to smile, if only a little, and said, "Good. I was trying to decide which way to start looking, and now you can carry me there."

"Crows are lazy creatures," said Oak. There was something sad in the great owl's voice. "You would have been better suited as an owl."

The Crow Girl frowned, slow as sunset in the summer. "I don't know what you mean."

"No," said Oak. "You wouldn't."

The great red owl flew on and on, until the fog began to lift, until the Crow Girl could see the towering tops of broad-branched trees. They were tall, twisting trees, made up of dozens of gently curving branches as thick around as a grown man's leg, weaving in and out of their vast canopy as they formed a lattice of leaves and boughs and bowers, each one sweetly inviting. Oak flew on, and the Crow Girl saw the land appear around the trees, fertile and flowering, ripe with fields yearning for the harvest. Everything looked good, and warm, and welcoming, and for no reason she could name, the Crow Girl began to cry.

She was still crying when Oak came gliding into the canopy itself, dropping her into a nest woven from grasses and willow boughs before taking a place on one of the twisted branches, right between Meadowsweet and Broom.

"You're here!" cried Zib in delight, slinging her arms around the Crow Girl's neck.

Avery was more subdued. He waved shyly with his free hand; the other was occupied by holding tight to a piece of flavor fruit, a hole already gnawed in the rind.

And there, sitting a few feet away, in a small puddle of water that had rolled off her skin and clothing, was Niamh. She smiled at the sight of the Crow Girl.

"I knew they would find you," she said.

"I thought *we* were looking for *you*," said the Crow Girl.

"Everything is more than one thing, if you look at it the right way," said Niamh.

The Crow Girl laughed, bright and merry. "Then

here we are, and there you are, and we're all together again! What a beautiful, beautiful day!"

"Together, and in the protectorate of the Queen of Wands," said Meadowsweet. The great blue owl fluffed her feathers out, almost doubling in size. "We can't stay here for long. We're each of us banned from this place, for one reason or another."

"None of them important now," said Broom. "You made it almost to the border before we intervened."

"So why intervene at all?" asked Avery. "We could have followed the road. We could have—"

"Your companions have not deceived you intentionally," said Broom. "They have told you the truth as they know it, and if that truth failed to serve you top to bottom, side to side, that was less fault and more failure. No one can reveal what they don't know. Please don't blame them."

"But deception is still deception," said Oak, picking up the thread smoothly. "And the lie would not have turned to truth at the border. Did you not wonder why, when the Queen of Swords had promised you passage, that same passage placed you precisely where you didn't want to be? Where you *couldn't* safely be?"

"There are always obstacles in the Up-and-Under," said Meadowsweet. "What is a journey without obstacles? A meal must have variety; a year must change its weather. But those obstacles are rarely so close to deadly. You have been tried, and tried, and tried, and every trial has been set with the sole purpose of slowing your steps long enough for your journey to be ended. Why do you think that might have been?"

Zib and Avery exchanged a look. Turning back to the owls, Zib ventured, "Because there are a lot of monsters in the Up-and-Under, and children are delicious?"

"She has a point there," said the Crow Girl. "My old friend the Bumble Bear says that children are *definitely* delicious."

"I don't think people are supposed to be food," said Avery. "Please don't eat us."

"They were trying to keep you from reaching the border," said Oak. "The improbable road has one job: to go from wherever it is to the borders of the Impossible City. It doesn't care about dynasties, or successions, or anything so trivial as who sits upon a throne."

"It would have led you right into the guards," said Broom. "It would have carried on without you, leaving you to face the consequences."

"So the Up-and-Under has been . . . trying to protect us?" asked Zib.

"The Up-and-Under doesn't care that much about you," said Meadowsweet regretfully. "The Up-and-Under protects itself first, and its people second, and visitors like yourselves last of all. The Up-and-Under has been trying to keep you from knowing what you shouldn't know."

"If we're not supposed to know this, why are you telling us?" asked Avery.

"Countries are curious things, and kingdoms are simply countries in their dancing shoes," said Oak.

"They think wide and long and slow. Sometimes, we need things to be narrow and short and swift, if they're to come to anything worth having."

"The Queen of Wands is missing," said Broom. "She's been missing for some time."

"She vanished from her receiving hall, when she should have been attending on her people," said Meadowsweet. "If the Kings know, if the other Queen knows, they've not told anyone, which makes us think they don't know, because they would never keep such a powerful secret. All of them want to take the Impossible City for their very own. All of them want to wear the crystal crown and hold the diamond scales and rule all that can be seen. Only the one who took her knows, and that one holds their cards closely, for it's possible to rule in secret only when uncontested."

"I don't understand," said Zib.

"You can't go home," said Niamh. "You're exiles now. Like me."

Avery and Zib turned to look at her, eyes wide and bewildered. Niamh smiled wanly.

"The improbable road will lead you to the Impossible City, but only the Queen of Wands can show you how to go back where you were before you came here," she said. "The other monarchs could help you, and the King of Coins *might*, if you could pay his price, but the others never would, because keeping you would be so much more profitable for them. So you'll stay, and stay, and stay, until we find her, until we bring her home."

Avery dropped his fruit and stared at her. Zib

hugged her knees to her chest with one arm, touching the sword by her side with her other hand. Neither of them spoke.

The Crow Girl was not so restrained. "That can't be right!" she cried. "The Queen is in her parlor, the light is in the tower, and all is right with the world! All is right, because otherwise, all would be wrong, and I . . . I . . . I don't know what to do in a world where the Queen of Wands is missing!"

"None of us do," said Oak. "But we know you can find the way. We know you can find her, if you look. Please." The great owl swiveled to face the children. "Please find our Queen. If you bring her back to the Impossible City, then anything you ask for will be yours."

"Even the way home," said Broom.

"Forever," said Meadowsweet.

"But . . ." Zib looked at Avery, then at the Crow Girl, and finally back to the owls. "We're just kids! We can't find your Queen! We can't even find our *shoes*!"

"I told you bare feet were better," said the Crow Girl smugly, and Avery, startled, laughed.

"You did," he said. "You really did." He turned to Oak. "Why does it have to be us?"

"You're new here," said the owl. "You don't know what's possible and what isn't. You'll take chances and take risks and make guesses that no one who understands the Up-and-Under would think of, because the rules aren't a part of you."

"You're clever," said Broom. "Both of you, in different ways, and you trust each other, even when you think you don't. You'll hold fast to one another, and where one of you goes, the other will follow, again and again, until the question's answered."

"You're all we have," said Meadowsweet. She shook her feathers, looking at them with large, sad eyes. "If there were anything else to be done, we might do it, for I do not care for leaving children to do our duties. But there is nothing else, and there is no one else, and the Impossible City will fall if it is not kept, and the Impossible City must not fall. Do you understand? Please, do you understand?"

"I do," said Zib.

"I do," said Avery.

"I don't," said the Crow Girl, and cawed harsh laughter. "But I guess I'll stay anyway. Children need to be watched over, and I can watch a dozen things at the same time."

"Then go," said Oak. "Find her. We'll be waiting."

The owls rose up in unison, silent wings spread wide as they soared away from the tree, leaving the children, and the Crow Girl, behind.

Avery wrinkled his nose. "I hate heights," he said.

"Oh, heights are easy," said the Crow Girl. "It's falling that's hard." She beamed, briefly, before bursting into birds and flying away.

Zib was the next to move. She grabbed her sword and stood, looking at the jungle gym of branches around them for a moment before she laughed and began swinging herself down.

There was nothing after that but for Avery and Niamh

to follow or be left behind. They descended with the careful slowness of children who have always preferred there be something beneath their feet, whether it be water or earth. When they reached the bottom, Zib was already tangled in a large berry-bush, her fingers and lips sticky with juice, while the crows swirled around her, stripping fruit from the highest branches. She turned, waving, and the crows came together into the body of the Crow Girl, feathers smoothing into place.

"Are we ready to go?" asked Zib.

"We are," said Avery, and so they did.

THIRTEEN

THE IMPOSSIBLE CITY

The first thing was to find the improbable road, which was at once easier and harder than it sounded. Most roads, being stationary, well-behaved things, are simply impossible to find in a place where they do not customarily go. The road that leads from the woods to Grandmother's house, for instance, cannot be found in a city or town, or on a seashore, or spanning a mountain. It begins in one place, always, and ends in another place, always. Had that been the road they were seeking, they would certainly never have been able to find it, and would have spent the rest of their days walking confused circles in a place that could never help them to fulfill their quests.

There are, however, other roads, moving roads, roads

made of cause and concept rather than cobblestone and convenience. The improbable road knew its travelers, and wanted, in its slow, architectural way, to help them.

One by one, the children set their bare feet on the grassy ground. Avery slipped his hand into Zib's, not flinching from the berry stains on her fingers, while Niamh walked a little bit apart, her feet leaving puddles behind her as she walked. The Crow Girl circled them all, walking great loops around them, so that they were always in her line of sight. She kept one eye on the sky, and no one asked her why. None of them wanted to know.

If this were a story about an ordinary sort of place, crisscrossed with ordinary sorts of road, we could follow them forever, three children and a gangling teenage girl walking under a sapphire sky, heading for the horizon. But this is not that kind of story. Zib glanced down, and saw a glimmer between her toes, like fireflies caught under the grass. She gasped. Avery looked down and did the same.

"The improbable road!" Zib said.

"Keep walking," urged the Crow Girl. "It's figuring out where we were!"

They kept walking, and the grass grew thinner under their feet, the glitter of the improbable road showing through more and more clearly, until the grass was gone and they were walking on glittering stones, walking toward the top of a gentle rise, its slopes peppered with brightly colored flowers. The Crow Girl stopped her circling and fell back to walk by Avery's side, so that they formed a line: first Niamh, then Zib, then Avery, and finally the Crow Girl, all of them walking in easy harmony.

They crested the rise, and there, before them, was the Impossible City.

The first impossibility was this: it was impossible that they had not been able to see it from a distance, for it was made of towers and spires and twisting, delicate peaks, all of them straining toward the sky like they thought to pierce the sun, to harness the moon. Clouds skittered among their peaks, tangling on balconies and obscuring windows.

The second impossibility was this: it was impossible for a city of such vast size and complexity to exist without changing the land around it, yet the Impossible City—surrounded by a wall of glittering, glistening stone, like a loop of the improbable road had somehow been coaxed into standing on its side—rose whole and shining out of field and farmland. There were no scattered settlements, no clear-cut forests, no quarries. It could have been conjured out of the earth already constructed, complete and unchangeable, pristine and perfect.

Avery and Zib stood hand-in-hand, looking at the great towers of the Impossible City, their mouths hanging open and their eyes filled with wonders. The buildings here weren't like any other buildings they had ever seen. They *moved*, changing shape and form and function according to the needs of the people who walked on their high terraces, moving between the buildings like dreams. Stairways formed and came apart; bridges danced themselves into existence and back out of it again.

Beside them, Niamh sighed.

"What's wrong?" asked Zib.

"I lived here once," said Niamh. "I never will again."

"Why not?"

"Because drowned girls are very possible, and the Impossible City only welcomes impossible things. Girls like me happen too often to ever make it our home." Niamh shook her head. "It is a fine and lovely and glorious place to live. It is kinder than it needs to be, and cruel enough to be real. But it isn't mine anymore, and it won't be tomorrow, or the day after that."

"That doesn't matter," said Zib stubbornly. "If it's not your home, it won't be our home, either. You can come back over the wall with us. We have a guest room, and my mother won't care if you get the sheets all wet. You can stand in her garden and water it without doing anything, and she'll call you her favorite and bake you all the cookies you want."

Avery, whose mother *would* have minded a perpetually damp houseguest, said, "We're not going there anyway, not now. The improbable road will have to take us somewhere else. No one goes home if we don't find the Queen of Wands."

"I haven't got a home to go to," said the Crow Girl. "I gave it away, wherever it was, when I gave my name to the King of Cups. I don't remember anything about it, except that it was beautiful, and I loved it very much, and I had to leave."

"Why?" asked Zib.

"I don't remember that, either." The corner of the Crow Girl's mouth quirked upward. "Awful, isn't it? I must have been very frightened, to give so many things away without getting anything but feathers in return. I like my feathers well enough. I might have liked a feather bed even more, once upon a time that I've forgotten."

"It's better to forget a home than to lose it," said Niamh.

The Crow Girl looked at her. "Is it?" she asked.

Niamh didn't have an answer.

The sky was finally growing darker, the sun dipping low on the distant line of the horizon. Avery dropped Zib's hand in order to shade his eyes, looking around.

"If we can't go to the city, we need to find a place to spend the night," he said. "We'll start looking for the Queen of Wands in the morning."

Zib nodded. "Where will we go?"

"Anywhere you want. Adventures follow the people who are having them."

"Will you stay with me?"

Avery reached for Zib's hand again. She let him take it, and they tangled their fingers together like the roots of a tree, so tight that they might never come apart.

"Always," he said.

They turned away from the great, glittering jewel of the Impossible City, Niamh and the Crow Girl by their sides. They started to walk.

The improbable road was there to meet them.

EPILOGUE

IN WHICH TWO CHILDREN ARE MISSING

In the same ordinary town, on the same ordinary street, two ordinary households were watching the sidewalk with fear and trepidation. They were waiting for their children—their ordinary, everyday, predictable children—to come home. They had been waiting for hours. They felt like they had been waiting for years.

How surprised they would have been, those children, if they had been able to see the fear on their parents' faces, the way they scanned the distance in every possible direction, the way their hands shook as they held tightly to whatever they could find! It was easy to believe their parents had other concerns to keep them occupied. Nothing could have been further from the truth.

Unaware of how far their children had gone, or how far they had left to go, their parents watched, and waited, and hoped for a quick and easy ending, the sort of tidy thing that only ever comes in stories, and so rarely graces us here, in the real world, where real costs can be incurred, and real prices must be paid.

They would be waiting for a very long time.